BLOOD FLIES UPWARDS

'What do you think happened, then?'

'I'm as much in the dark as you are. We've had only one idea, my brother and I, and most of the time it seems to me quite fantastic. But just sometimes it seems the only possible explanation. It's that Sally discovered something about the Eckersalls, something very dangerous to them, and that frightened them so badly that they – they got rid of her.'

'Murdered her.'

'I find it awfully difficult to say that word.'

'You may have to face it sooner or later.'

'I know.'

'And just what are you hoping to achieve here yourself?'

'I came because, if she found out this thing, perhaps I can find it out too and use it to make them tell us what happened to her.'

'If they don't decide to get rid of you too. Have you thought of that?'

'I'm afraid I think about it nearly all the time.'

**Also by the same author,
and available from Coronet:**

Blood Flies Upwards

Elizabeth Ferrars

CORONET BOOKS
Hodder and Stoughton

Copyright © 1976 by M. D. Brown

First published in Great Britain in 1976 by William Collins Sons & Co. Ltd.
Reissued in 1990 by Constable & Company Ltd.
Coronet edition 1992

British Library C.I.P.

A CIP catalogue record for this title is available from the British Library

ISBN 0-340-56397-4

Printed and bound in Great Britain for Hodder and Stoughton Paperbacks, a division of Hodder and Stoughton Ltd., Mill Road, Dunton Green, Sevenoaks, Kent TN13 2YA (Editorial Office: 47 Bedford Square, London WC1B 3DP) by Clays Ltd., St Ives plc.

CHAPTER I

THE TAXI STOPPED outside an archway through which Alison could see a wide courtyard with tall buildings round it and a big, circular flowerbed in the centre, filled with wondrously blooming pink rhododendrons. A single jet of water sprang up out of the flowerbed, falling back in a delicate curve into the basin from which it arose and forming a dazzling little rainbow in the May-time sunshine. The courtyard had a number of cars parked in it, which without exception were large and expensive.

Alison paid the taxi-driver and advanced diffidently through the archway. Money in large quantities always made her feel diffident. And however little the plain façades of the tall buildings told you about the people who lived in these flats, there was one thing of which you could be certain, they were all very wealthy.

Or it might be, she thought, that they were only playing at being wealthy, living on hope and large overdrafts. But this was an ability that amazed and intimidated her even more than solid riches. And even if some of them, and of course it was the Eckersalls that she had in mind, were not quite what they seemed, they must at least be the kind of people who would appear convincingly the right sort of tenants to inhabit a flat in such a luxurious hive.

This distrustful thought was not characteristic of Alison. Normally she was not a distrustful person. But there was something about what she had set herself to do that day which had persuaded her that for once in her life she had to be cautious, must listen for the false note in the un-likeliest of voices and watch for pretence even where there seemed to be nothing but courtesy and naturalness.

It was a state of mind that caused her an almost physical discomfort, which she realized was at bottom a kind of fear. Fear simply because she was about to be false herself, to play a part, and she had next to no confidence in her ability to do it successfully.

There was an entrance at each corner of the courtyard, with three wide semicircular steps leading up to each doorway. The entrance for which she was looking was the farther one on the left. The board beside it showed that the flats to which the door gave access were Nos. 40–60. She went inside into a pale marble lobby with a lift facing her across it.

The lift was automatic, but before she could reach it a porter emerged from a doorway beside it and asked her with dignity what flat she wanted. She told him that she wanted Mrs Eckersall's. He said that was on the fourth floor, opened the doors of the lift for her, showed her which button to press and let the doors close.

Murmuring thanks and meeting his eyes, assessing her through the closing grille, she felt a moment of blind panic. Until then she had had the feeling that she could turn back if she chose, admitting to herself that she had been playing a kind of game all along and had never been really serious. But now that had become impossible. Once the lift had started to ascend she simply could not press the button to take her down to the ground floor again to plunge out through the archway and past that calm-faced but interested man who would certainly remember her.

The lift came to a gentle stop at the fourth floor. She got out, closed the doors behind her and went along the passage to No. 49.

For a moment after she had rung the bell she heard nothing inside the flat, then suddenly, without there having been any sound of approaching footsteps, the door was jerked open. It was done with a kind of impatience, as if she were late and had been keeping the woman who stood there waiting unpardonably. But it was just four o'clock, the time of their appointment. Alison had been careful to be punctual to the minute.

'Mrs Goodrich?' the woman said.

When Alison answered yes, the woman thrust out a hand, then used her grip to haul Alison through the door, slamming it shut behind her, almost as if she were being taken into custody. But the truth of it, she thought, was merely that for some reason Mrs Eckersall was extremely nervous, taut with worries of her own of which at that time Alison knew nothing, which made all her movements jerky and over-forceful. She walked ahead of Alison into a big sitting-room. The reason that her approach to the door when Alison rang had been noiseless was that she was barefooted and her footfalls made no sound on the deep carpet.

She had rather large feet, but they were well-shaped and muscular. She was tall and wide-shouldered and looked about forty years old. She was wearing black trousers and a tight black and silver blouse with balloon-like sleeves and an upstanding collar. She had several chains of many-coloured beads round her neck and an enormous flashing diamond ring on one finger. Her hands, like her feet, were large and strong and shapely.

With an abrupt gesture she pointed at where Alison was to sit on a stiff, pretty little Victorian chair, then she sat down facing her on a long, low, bulbous couch covered in black corduroy and smothered in bright cushions. Pulling her knees up to her chin and folding her arms round them, she gave Alison one hard look, then frowned down at her toes, wriggling them a little.

She was a striking-looking woman. Her hair was of a

very pale shade of gold and was piled up high on her head. Her face was a triangle, wide at her temples and with rather stony grey eyes set far apart under finely arched dark eyebrows. She had a short, narrow, arrogant nose, a wide mouth that did not go with the eyes because it had a generous, humorous line to it, and a sharply pointed chin. A puzzling face and full of contradictions, as Alison took in even in their first few minutes of conversation.

'All right, you're a friend of Linda Prentice's,' Mrs Eckersall said in a deep voice that had an odd, not unfriendly rasp in it. 'But I don't understand. You don't look the type for the job.'

'I thought, when Linda said she'd left, it sounded just right for me,' Alison answered.

'Why?'

'Well . . .'

She had been trying to get used to the room, which was as full of contradictions as Mrs Eckersall's face. It looked as if someone had made a rush job of buying a lot of simple Scandinavian furniture, then had had an orgy at Sotheby's, buying costly and very ornate antiques. The general effect was one of restless confusion. Alison felt that whoever had assembled these things did not really care for any of them. The pictures were fiercely abstract. They said nothing to her, but abstracts never did, so she made no attempt to appraise them. Perhaps they were excellent.

'Well, I can cook,' she said.

'Who can't, nowadays? But you don't look the kind of person who'd make a career of it. How old are you?'

'Twenty-seven.'

'Well, you look – I don't know how to put it – too sophisticated, is that what I mean? You're obviously well educated. You've probably got a degree.'

Alison had not been prepared for this kind of direct-ness. She thought that she had dressed in a very unsophis-ticated way that day. She was wearing a jersey suit which had once been good and to which she clung, but which was at least three years old, had put on flat-heeled brown walking shoes and was carrying a bulging, untidy-looking handbag. She had brushed her dark hair straight back from her face and tucked it neatly behind her ears and had on next to no make-up.

'I *have* got a degree,' she admitted.

'In what subject?'

'Biochemistry. But that was five years ago, so what I know is hopelessly out of date already. Things move so fast. I don't suppose it would get me a job now and it happens that the sooner I can get one the better.'

'But you're married,' Mrs Eckersall said. 'Why do you need a job so badly?'

Alison said nothing.

'Something went wrong, did it?' All of Mrs Eckersall's questions came suddenly, as if she hardly knew herself what she was likely to say next.

'He left me,' Alison answered.

'How long ago?'

'A few weeks. Do you mind if we don't talk about it?'

But the other woman persisted. 'He left you without any money?'

'No, I'm not actually short of money yet,' Alison said. 'But it's staying alone in that place, that flat, having nothing to do when I get up, starting to think, starting to feel . . . Please, I really don't want to talk about it. We haven't decided what we mean to do about the future. But meanwhile, I've realized, I've simply got to find something to do. And when I met Linda Prentice at a friend's house at the weekend and she told me about the job she'd left, I thought just possibly you might be ready to take me on. So I telephoned.' She risked a smile. 'I really can cook.'

Mrs Eckersall did not respond to the smile. Stretching out her legs on the deep black couch, she went on gazing absently at her own bare toes.

'The bitch left us without a day's notice,' she said. 'Just packed her bags and went, only ringing up to say she found the job too lonely. Did she tell you that – that the job was lonely? If it's companionship you're needing now it isn't going to be much use to you.'

'It isn't really companionship I'm looking for,' Alison said. 'It's more just something to do – I mean something I've *got* to do. Not simply to have an empty day ahead of me, with no obligations to anybody – no need even to get up in the morning if I can't be bothered.'

'But you won't stay with us long, will you, if that's the case? As soon as you've sorted out your own problems, you'll leave. That's obvious.'

'I suppose I can't promise anything about that, but wouldn't a stop-gap be useful?'

Frowning, Mrs Eckersall muttered, 'I never did like that girl, you know. One weekend she tells me how happy she is and only a few days later she telephones me she can't stand it because she's so lonely and she's off back to London. Can you imagine doing a thing like that? She'd only stuck it for a fortnight.'

The truth was that Alison could easily imagine Mrs Eckersall acting just as Linda Prentice was said to have done. If this woman felt bored or lonely she would act swiftly on whatever impulse seemed to promise a solution of her own difficulties, without much consideration for the comfort of others.

Mrs Eckersall went on, 'Is she a close friend of yours?'

'I hardly know her,' Alison said. 'As I told you, I met her in a friend's house and she talked about the job she'd left and I suddenly had the idea that it was just the kind of thing I needed. So I got your name and address from her and telephoned you the same evening. If you want references . . .'

Mrs Eckersall stopped her with a wave of the hand with the flashing ring on it.

'I don't trust references. Anyone can fake them. That Prentice girl had a parcel of references and look how much they meant. I prefer to trust my instincts. I can tell a lot from people's faces. Yours is honest, though you're hiding something, aren't you? Something about that husband of yours, perhaps. Are you hoping to get him back?'

Alison could feel the flush mount in her face. She found it disturbing to be called honest just then.

Seeing the flush, Mrs Eckersall laughed.

'All right, you don't want to talk about it. And why should you? It's not my business. But I want to be sure you understand just what the job is. We want someone who'll take care of our house in the country for us. It's near Helsington, which is quite a nice little town, but we're about three miles out of it in real country, which is pleasant if you like it, but of course some people don't. Which reminds me, you can drive, I suppose?'

Alison nodded.

'Because you'd need the car to do the shopping. The house isn't particularly large and you'd have no housework to do, because a Mrs Rumbold comes in every morning except Sunday to do the cleaning. You'd simply have to keep an eye on things generally, then do the shopping and cooking at the weekends when my husband and I come down. Sometimes we bring friends and we give the odd party now and then, but mostly we live very quietly when we're down there. And we like quite simple food. You wouldn't find the job difficult. You'd have a sort of little flatlet to yourself, with your own bathroom and television and so on. Wages, now . . .'

So the first step had been accomplished. Alison had the job. Some of the tension went out of her. When Mrs Eckersall told her what she had been paying Linda Prentice, Alison said that that seemed quite satisfactory.

'Then when can you start?' Mrs Eckersall asked.

'Tomorrow, if you like.'

'Tomorrow!' Mrs Eckersall gave a little laugh to which the rasp in her voice gave a peculiarly sardonic sound. 'You really are keen to get away from that flat of yours, aren't you? Will you tell your husband where you've gone, I wonder. But we don't talk about that, do we? Yes, tomorrow would be fine, and if you get there in the morning Mrs Rumbold would be at the house and would have time to show you round and get you settled in before we come down on Friday. But listen, are you sure you aren't going to mind being in a fairly solitary place and won't start getting frightened when Mrs Rumbold's gone and you're all alone and it gets dark?' Her eyes were on Alison's face, bold, exploratory, summarizing. 'Because if you aren't quite sure of that, for God's sake tell me now and drop the whole thing. I'm tired of being let down.'

Alison told her that she was sure that she would not suffer from any serious irrational fears of being alone in a house in the country.

'Good,' Mrs Eckersall said. 'I like being alone myself. Sometimes I wish I had more of it. Of course, if you run into trouble of any kind, there's always Barry Jones. He's our gardener and he lives in a flat over the garage. He won't bother you at all, he's very nice and quiet. But if a fuse needs mending or something goes wrong with the car or anything of that sort, he can always cope. So that's settled, isn't it? You'll go down tomorrow.'

'Thank you,' Alison said. 'I'm glad you think I'll do.'

'As to that,' Mrs Eckersall said, 'time will tell. My

present feeling is, will *I* do? Linda isn't the only one to have walked out on me, you know. There was another girl before her. Yet I honestly don't think I'm difficult to get on with. I interfere as little as I can. And for God's sake, if you're unhappy about anything, just tell me. You wouldn't say I'm difficult to talk to, would you? If you're dissatisfied in any way, if you have trouble with Mrs Rumbold or anything, just come to me and tell me about it and we'll see what we can work out.'

She swung her feet down to the carpet with one of the sudden movements that gave her the look of not knowing in advance where she was going, and stood up, unfolding herself into someone even taller than Alison remembered from when she had come in.

'I wouldn't have said that to just anybody,' Mrs Eckersall went on, 'but I think you'll know what I mean. I don't mean that you should come to me with every minor grievance. I'll expect you to be able to manage those by yourself. Now if you're serious about going down tomorrow, there's a good train at eleven-ten, which gets you to Helsington about half past twelve. I'll tell Barry to meet it. And I'll telephone Mrs Rumbold and tell her to get a room ready for you and get in some food so that you needn't rush off to the shops straight away. Or you can help yourself out of the freezer if you'd sooner. Well?'

'The eleven-ten,' Alison said. 'Yes, I can manage that.'

Rather wonderingly Mrs Eckersall observed, 'You know, I've got a strange feeling this is going to work out, for a while anyway, though I didn't think so when I first saw you. We'll meet again on Friday. I hope you'll feel quite at home by then.'

'Thank you.'

Mrs Eckersall gave another sardonic little laugh. Alison was not sure what it meant, whether she was laughing at Alison's pretences, which she had seen through all too easily, or at a certainty that Alison had seen through some of hers. For Alison was sure that the other woman was not at all the easy-going, considerate person that she had been trying to make herself out to be. She was something much more complex than that.

But did that matter to either of them, so long as they had come to an understanding of a kind?

Mrs Eckersall saw Alison to the door and stood there, a gawkily impressive, almost beautiful woman, until she had seen the lift descending.

The porter who had seen Alison come in watched her go out, renewing her feeling that if ever she should have reason to return, he would know her again. The people who lived in these flats were carefully watched over. She went out past the great bed of rhododendrons and through the archway into the street. She paused there, uncertain whether to wait, hoping for a taxi to come along, or walk a couple of hundred yards to the nearest bus stop.

She decided on the bus, less from economy, though that was not unimportant, than from a feeling of needing to walk off what she still felt of the tension that had kept her so monosyllabic in Mrs Eckersall's flat. She supposed that Mrs Eckersall had taken note of it, for those rather blind-looking, granite-grey eyes had seemed to Alison more than usually observant. But she hoped that her stiff quiet had been attributed to her anxiety to get the job, or perhaps to the devastation caused to her nervous system by her broken marriage.

She walked fast, then had to wait for a quarter of an hour before the bus that she wanted came along. A woman behind her in the bus queue had been complaining that getting about London was becoming more and more impossible, then tried to board the bus ahead of Alison, who jabbed an elbow into her ribs in a mean sort of way and scrambled up before her. That made her feel better.

She had been holding herself in so tightly for the last half-hour that a little bit of ill-mannered aggression was just what she needed.

The bus took her to Battersea to a stop only a few minutes' walk from her brother's flat. There was no porter there and no lift. Concrete steps led up from landing to landing and the walls, of dingy cream, were in bad need of re-painting. Geoffrey and Katrina lived on the third floor. As soon as Alison rang the bell she heard Geoffrey's footsteps come hurrying to the door and when he saw her he flung an arm round her and held her close for a moment.

'God, I've been worrying!' he said. 'Of course, the whole scheme's mad. But you've been, haven't you? Which of them did you see?'

'The woman, naturally,' Alison answered. 'It's the wife who normally appoints the domestic staff.'

Geoffrey's long bony arms dropped to his sides. He was looking even more dishevelled than usual, with his straight fair hair standing up, well raked by his restless fingers, and his thin face flushed, as if, early in the evening as it was, he had already had several drinks. In the narrow little passage of the flat he seemed to tower over Alison even more than usual. He was wearing a white shirt, none too fresh, unbuttoned at the neck, and the dark grey trousers that went with his office suit. He worked in advertising with a success that she had never expected of him, for he was only twenty-five, yet he was already earning more than her husband, Mark, ever had in his life.

'What did you make of her?' Geoffrey asked.

'She said I looked too sophisticated for the job, but I don't think she actually suspected anything.'

Alison squeezed past him to look at herself in the long mirror that hung on the wall at the end of the passage. She herself could see no signs of sophistication. It seemed to her that she looked plain and rather fierce. It struck her that if she had been Mrs Eckersall she would probably not have given this person a job.

'Perhaps she meant you sounded too sophisticated,' Geoffrey said. 'Wrong sort of voice, wrong sort of accent.'

'You seem to be taking for granted I got the job,' Alison said.

'Of course you did. If you hadn't, you'd have said so by now. When does it start?'

'Tomorrow.'

He looked dismayed. 'That's pushing it, isn't it? I mean, do you want to seem too eager?'

'I don't see why not. She was eager enough to have me start at once.'

'Come in then and have a drink. You look as if you need one.'

'I do. Whisky, please, with very little water.'

They went into the sitting-room where the drinks were set out waiting for them on a tray on a coffee table. Geoffrey's glass, half full, was on the floor beside a chair. The room was small, untidy, undistinguished and friendly. Alison stretched out comfortably on the shabby sofa, glad of the change from that other disturbing room.

As he poured out a drink for her and topped up his own, Geoffrey said, 'You told her the Prentice woman told you the job was going, did you?' Then he raised his voice and called, 'Katrina, do you want a drink? Alison's here.'

A voice answered faintly from the kitchen.

'Yes, I told her we'd met in a friend's house,' Alison said. 'That was one of the only real lies I had to tell. She didn't ask me much.'

'What did you tell her about Mark?'

'That he'd left me.'

'You don't call that a real lie?'

'Well, it isn't, is it?' The whisky was warming her, driving out the chill from which she had suffered the whole afternoon. She began to feel pleased with the way that she had conducted the affair. 'She wasn't at all what I expected. Linda Prentice gave me the impression of a foul-tempered kind of creature who'd fly off the handle if ever you answered back. But she seemed particularly anxious to be friendly. Not that I exactly trusted that.'

'You may discover the foul temper when you get to know her better.'

The door was flung open and Katrina darted in. The smell of some exotic dish was wafted in after her from the kitchen. She was a small, slight, very serious girl who taught in a school for the physically handicapped, work which utterly absorbed her so that her housekeeping was inevitably very haphazard and yet was curiously agreeable in its results. That casserole in the oven, for instance, would certainly be delicious. She had long fair hair, as fine as a young child's, and a flowerlike softness of skin. She looked extremely fragile though in fact her energy was all but inexhaustible. Her big grey eyes were normally gently earnest, but now they looked anxious and excited.

'You haven't really done it!' she exclaimed, throwing herself down on the sofa close to Alison and clutching her arm. 'I never believed you were really going to.'

'But I have,' Alison said, 'and I've got the job.'

'Oh no! Oh, I wish you hadn't! I know it's a fearful mistake. I can feel it. I can feel some terrible thing is going to happen.'

Katrina came from the West Highlands and was given to trusting her premonitions. She had never quite convinced Alison that they were any more reliable than those of anyone else, but she knew that it gave Katrina pleasure to believe that there was something special about them. It made her feel different from other people, quietly, brilliantly gifted.

'Perhaps,' she went on with great agitation, 'it will be even worse than what's happened already. If that's possible. Alison darling, it's a great shock to me that you're really going to that place.'

Geoffrey poured her out a very stiff whisky and water. She would probably have two or three more before the evening was out without showing any signs of having had them. She had an extraordinary tolerance of alcohol.

'Did that Mrs Eckersall talk about the dreadful gardener?' she asked. 'The one that frightened Linda Prentice so badly.'

'The Prentice girl's a fool,' Geoffrey said. 'She thought just because he once had a mental breakdown he was going to rape her or murder her. But did Mrs Eckersall say anything about him, Alison?'

'Only that he lived in a flat over the garage and was nice and quiet and would mend fuses. He's going to meet me at the station tomorrow.'

'Oh, oh, oh!' Katrina wailed. 'It's all a great mistake. She didn't want to put you off by telling you anything about him. He may really be insane and dangerous. He may be at the bottom of everything. You know that. Ignorant people like Linda Prentice often have a great deal of insight. But listen, Alison, you must telephone us very often. Every day. Every evening when we've both got home from work. If you don't we'll get sick with worry.'

'I don't think that sounds very practical,' Alison said. 'The Eckersalls may have objections to my using their telephone for too many private calls.'

'Then you can go a little walk down to the village and telephone from the post office there.'

'I'm not sure if there is a village. Mrs Eckersall talked as if the house was very solitary.'

'So it is, fairly,' Geoffrey said. 'There are a few houses

dotted about, but I can't remember anything you'd call a village.'

'And anyway, those regular arrangements are never a good idea,' Alison said. 'If some small thing stopped me making a call when you expected it, you'd start really worrying when there might be no need for it.'

'I think you're right.' Geoffrey was looking sombre, as if he regretted the whole plan that they had made, although in the beginning it had been his idea. But Alison was used to that in him. He was always full of ideas which he never expected to have carried out and he was sometimes badly shaken if they showed signs of developing into reality. 'All the same, telephone pretty often, will you? You'll have the place to yourself except at weekends. You ought to be able to manage it somehow.'

'I could tell Mrs Eckersall I've got a sick relative,' Alison suggested, 'and offer to pay for all the calls I feel I ought to make.'

He shook his head. 'Don't tell any more lies than you've got to. They're a great strain on the memory. The nearer you can stick to the truth about all the minor things, the less likely you are to get muddled about the important ones.'

'It's all wrong, you shouldn't be going,' Katrina said. 'But I know you won't listen to me. You and Geoffrey are so alike, you're both stubborn and irresponsible. Now you'll stay to dinner with us. It's pork chops in cider. I did an extra couple, knowing you'd be staying.'

'But if you don't mind, I think I'll go home,' Alison said. 'I've got to think out what I want to take with me and get my packing done. And I'm really awfully tired.'

'Stay and eat, then I'll drive you home,' Geoffrey suggested. 'That can't be more tiring than cooking for yourself. And have another drink meanwhile.'

He had poured it out before she could stop him.

Not that she had really wanted to stop him. If she had gone home she would have made herself some scrambled eggs, had a bath, pottered about the flat in her dressing-gown, assembling the belongings that she wanted to take with her next day, watched television for a little while, then gone to bed. That was the sort of programme that she had been getting used to lately and normally she did not mind it much. But tonight the thought of the empty flat was more disturbing than usual and starting to do her packing, she thought, would be almost as frightening as the moment in the lift when it had started to ascend towards the Eckersalls' flat and she had suddenly realized that there was no escaping now. It would be one of those points of no return that occur so often in the lives of everyone, yet which, luckily for most people, generally pass unnoticed.

So she was glad to stay with Geoffrey and Katrina and to let Katrina talk of her work, which she did eagerly, as if she thought that making Alison think of something other than their private problems might induce her to change her plans for tomorrow. But as soon as they had had coffee she said again that she must go and Geoffrey, as he had promised, drove her home.

The flat in which she and Mark had lived for three years was on the edge of Hampstead Heath. It was on the ground floor of a rather dilapidated Victorian house, graceless in design but with pleasantly large rooms with tall windows and good, simple, marble fireplaces. Usually Alison was sufficiently content in the place. But this evening, in its emptiness, it seemed peculiarly bleak and unwelcoming. It was going to get along quite well without her, it seemed to say. It made no effort to hold her back.

When Geoffrey had gone she began her packing. She had no idea how long she was likely to stay at the Eckersalls', so it was hard to decide what clothes she ought to take. But she could always come back for more if it turned out that she had to stay longer than she expected. While she wandered about the bedroom, selecting, folding, packing, a photograph of Mark watched her from the dressing-table. It was one of those portraits the eyes of which follow you about wherever you go. At one point she paused for a little and met that penetrating gaze.

The photograph was a good one. The smile looked spontaneous, the tilt of the head, as if he were listening carefully to something that was being said to him, was characteristic. And in spite of the smile, the squareness of Mark's face gave him a certain gravity, a look of being thoughtful, reliable. Alison crossed to the dressing-table and laid the photograph face down on it. She did not want to find herself putting words into her husband's mouth, hearing him tell her while he watched her what he thought of what she was doing.

When she had finished her packing she had a bath. She made it deep and hot, poured in some bath oil and lay in it for a long time. Slowly she relaxed. It was amusing really, she thought, how few direct lies she had had to tell Mrs Eckersall. Almost everything that she had said had been false and yet, taken literally, had almost all of it been true. About Mark having left her, for instance. In fact he had gone on a botanical expedition and on some unspecified date would return, but for the time being at least it could be said that he had left her. She chuckled at her own cunning.

But the chuckle broke off abruptly and she sat up in the steaming water and started to soap herself with a kind of punitive fierceness as she thought of the reason behind all her actions that day. What was there amusing about the disappearance into thin air from her quiet job in the country of a sister, a younger sister, to whom she had felt

very close and for whom she had always felt responsible?
A disappearance which the police seemed to think merely
indicated that she had wanted to get away from her
family, and which her employers thought of only as an
inconvenience for themselves. What folly to have found
it amusing even for a moment.

CHAPTER II

THE STATION at Helsington was a bare, windswept place. On the morning when Alison arrived the sky was overcast and there was a feeling of damp in the air, as if at any moment the heavy, dingy clouds might empty themselves of the rain they were carrying.

She felt cold and depressed. She also felt remarkably alone, which was not a feeling that she had had to suffer often in her life, at least until the last few weeks. She felt a sense of futility as well, a conviction that she was not the right person to carry out the job that she had undertaken. She was not really at all an adventurous character. Danger did not exhilarate her in any way. Not that she could be sure that she was walking into danger, but she had not slept well the night before and her imagination had had time to daub dramatic colours all over the rather simple little plan that she and Geoffrey had made. So the immediate future looked lurid. Grasping her two suitcases and the same worn, bulging handbag that she had carried the day before, she made for the exit.

'Mrs Goodrich?'

A man was standing at the top of the stairs that led down to the street. Not many people had left the train at Helsington and it could not have been difficult for him to pick her out. He was a tall man of about thirty, gaunt and slightly stooping, with reddish hair curling over his collar and a drooping moustache. His face was hollow-cheeked, with high cheekbones under slanting, greenish eyes. Sharp, observant eyes, Alison thought at first, and yet there was something curiously closed about his face. After his first quick glance at her, which seemed to take her in from head to foot and which told him, so it appeared, all that he required to know of her, his expression became almost empty. A slight smile which lifted the corners of his mouth under the moustache brought hardly any life to it.

'I'm Barry Jones,' he said in a voice that had a Midlands flatness in it. 'Mrs Eckersall told me to meet you. The car's outside.'

He reached for her suitcases.

He was wearing jeans and a black, high-necked sweater with the sleeves pushed up above the elbows and as he took the cases Alison noticed that his arms, though thin, looked singularly muscular. It struck her too as soon as he began to move, going quickly ahead of her down the stairs to the barrier, that there was something deceptive about his gangling figure, for there was a lightness in his tread, an ease and a poise about him that she would not have expected, seeing him lounging at the head of the stairs.

The car was a battered, cream-coloured Vauxhall. He opened the door for her, tossed her cases on to the back seat, went round behind the car and thrust his long legs under the steering wheel.

'I'm told you can drive this thing,' he said as they started.

'I think so,' she answered.

'Any time you want me to do it for you, let me know,' he said. 'I'm the gardener. She probably told you that. But I look after the cars too and I don't mind running errands. Make out a list, I'll do the shopping for you any day.'

'Thank you,' she said.

'I hope you know what you're in for here.'

They were held up by lights in the main street of the town and he turned his head as he said it to give her another of those swift, assessing glances that seemed to take her in entirely all at once. Then the lights changed and they moved on.

'You mean that the place is solitary,' she said.

'Oh, it's not as solitary as all that. If you can drive you won't mind it.'

'Then what's the trouble?'

'Funny thing, I don't know,' he said. 'But the last two girls they took left in an awful hurry.'

'Two of them?'

'That's right.'

'And you don't know why?'

'No, each of them just up and went. Or so I was told. The first one was before my time, but I heard all about her from our Mrs Rumbold.'

'But you're happy here yourself?'

'Happy?' He said it as if the idea of happiness were something for which he felt a certain scorn. Then after a pause he went on, 'I suppose you could say so. Suits me well enough, anyhow. They leave me to myself mostly. I like that.'

'But you haven't been here long,' Alison said.

'Only three weeks, just about.'

'Whom did they have before you?'

'No one, to go by the state the place was in. I've only just got started, getting it into shape.'

'How long have they had the house?'

'Ask a lot of questions, don't you? Six months or so.'

They had turned out of the main street with its rather impressive Town Hall, its chain stores and its traffic jams, into a narrower street of seedy shops and squalid-looking pubs, mostly carved out of the ground floors of old houses, a street that led to a complicated crossroads, in the centre of which a tall clock stated immovably that the time was a quarter to four.

The road that they took beyond the clock soon led them into an area of blocks of old-fashioned flats, after which they came to the kind of semi-detached houses that were built in the thirties, and after them to more recently built bungalows, standing cheek by jowl in impeccable little gardens. After the bungalows the country began, but only tentatively at first, meadows and orchards appearing here and there between more and more scattered buildings. Then at last there were fewer buildings than fields. It was dull country, flat and without hills or streams, but fresh and green, with plenty of trees.

Barry Jones turned the car in at some open gates and drove up a straight drive towards a long white house. A big open garage faced the end of the drive. Over the garage were the windows of what was presumably the flat he occupied. It was reached by a short flight of stone steps, built on outside the garage. These were almost against the fence that separated the Eckersalls' garden from the garden next door, which was even more of a wilderness than that of the Eckersalls, with a big but decrepit Georgian house standing in the midst of it. So, in spite of what Alison had been told, she would have neighbours living quite close by. Unless the house was empty. But there were curtains at the windows, tattered-looking and some of them still drawn although it was past midday, yet indicating that the house was probably occupied.

The fence between the gardens was only a couple of strands of wire, looped from post to post, against which, on both sides, flowering shrubs had been planted in profusion, making an irregular kind of hedge. A rambler rose, which had developed into a thorny mass of briar, grew just at the foot of the steps leading up to the flat above the garage. The rose had been planted in the garden next door, but most of the bush hung over the fence. The Eckersalls' garden was about an acre in size. The white house stood at the back of it with a sweep of lawn in front which had recently been mown. Some flowerbeds looked as if Barry Jones had been giving them a good deal of attention during the few weeks that he had worked here.

He drove straight into the garage and, getting out of the car, lifted Alison's suitcases out of it and said, 'I'll take these up to your room. Mrs Rumbold's still here. She usually leaves around twelve o'clock, but she said she'd stay on today and show you round and tell you everything.'

He did not trouble to close the doors of the garage. Alison followed him out into the drive, noticing again his easy, long-legged stride as he went ahead of her.

The drive itself came to an end at the garage. Leading off to the left of it was a paved terrace which ran the length of the house, which had obviously once been two or three cottages that at some time had been turned into one. Perhaps they had once been labourers' cottages, belonging to the house next door. The windows were small, set deep in the white walls, which were chequered with an incredible quantity of black beams. The roof had been thatched very newly, with wire netting protecting it from the nesting of birds. The white of the walls and the black of the beams looked very raw and new. It could not have been long since a very thorough job of renovation, with no expense spared, had been done on the old building.

About half-way along the front of the house a porch projected from it. Barry Jones led the way to it, pushed the door open and called out, 'Hi, Mrs Rumbold!'

'All right, all right,' a voice answered from somewhere and after a moment a woman emerged from the door at the end of a passage and came tramping heavily towards them.

She was a big woman, dressed in a dark blue nylon

overall and red velvet bedroom slippers. Her thick grey hair had recently had a tight permanent wave and stood out in a frizz round her fleshy face. She had thick, heavy eyelids that half-covered bright, very inquisitive light blue eyes. She wore a good deal of make-up, including some bright pink lipstick which made her wide mouth look shiny and somehow avid.

'Mrs Goodrich?' she said. 'I'm Mrs Rumbold. Pleased to meet you. I've been keeping dinner for you. You'll be hungry, I expect. Barry can take your cases up for you and you can unpack later, unless you'd like a wash first. Barry can show you the way while I'm dishing up.'

Alison said that she would like a wash and Barry said, 'Come on then,' and picked up the cases which he had put down on the red tiles of the hall and led the way up the stairs.

They were steep and narrow and half-way up he said, 'Mind your head,' and Alison found herself having to duck to avoid a low beam. She had seldom seen so many beams in any one house. It was full of little dark corners too and steps in unexpected places. She thought it rather much of a good thing. She liked old houses but she also liked the feeling that she could walk upright in safety and need not move cautiously in case of spraining an ankle. And she liked light and spaciousness. But it struck her that this was exactly the right kind of country house for Mrs Eckersall, by which she meant that she had already decided that there was something spurious about both the house and the woman. It was the sort of house in which you could easily pretend that you had roots, yet the truth was that the only people who had ever really had roots here must have been some over-crowded, underpaid families of farm labourers, long dead and gone.

'Well, here you are,' Barry said, opening a door.

'Make yourself at home. And if you want me for anything, you'll generally find me in the garden. Don't let Mrs Rumbold push you around. She's all right but she's got an idea the house belongs to her, and Mrs Eckersall doesn't mind who runs things as long as she isn't bothered.'

He put Alison's cases down and went out.

The room into which he had shown her was a small one with a sloping ceiling, chintz curtains, a patchwork quilt on the bed, some convenient built-in cupboards, one easy chair and a television. A door opened out of the room into a small bathroom. The window overlooked the garden. Alison could see the drive and the gates from it and after a moment Barry Jones walking along the terrace towards the steps leading up to his flat.

She shed her jacket, had a wash, combed her hair and went downstairs.

Mrs Rumbold was at the foot of the stairs, waiting for her.

'This way,' she said and led Alison along the passage down which she had first appeared into a large, bright, modern kitchen. 'I'm not a fancy cook but I've made a nice stew and an apple tart, so you needn't bother much over your supper this evening. You'll be wanting to find your way about the house, I expect, and where everything's kept so that you'll know where you are by the time the family come down tomorrow.'

'Thank you,' Alison said, 'you're very kind.'

'You look sort of tired,' Mrs Rumbold said as she ladled stew out of a saucepan on to plates. 'You eat a good dinner, then have a rest. Take things calmly, don't rush at them. You're nervous, I expect, coming to a new job.'

'I am rather,' Alison agreed as they sat down at the table.

'You don't want to worry,' Mrs Rumbold said. 'They're

all right here. I've been working for them ever since they
moved in. That's nearly six months ago now and it's as
good a job as I've ever had. Stew all right, dear?'

'It's very good.'

It was rich and dark and if only she had had an appetite
Alison would probably have enjoyed it.

'Funny thing,' Mrs Rumbold went on, 'she doesn't
seem able to keep people, all except me. That's two girls
left her within a few weeks. And I couldn't tell you why,
because I've always found her easy to get along with.
She's got a bit of a temper, but if you take no notice it
soon blows over. That's the thing to do, let me tell you,
take no notice of it. She'll come to you presently and say
she's sorry and how it was all her nerves. Terrible nerves
she's got. Drinks too much, of course, and takes I don't
know how many pills. I don't approve of all those pills
they give you nowadays, but live and let live is what I
say. I thank God for my own good health and that I
don't need any of those things, and I never cared for
spirits, only my Guinness in the evening and a brandy
puff for a special occasion. Ever tried a brandy puff,
dear?'

'I don't think I have,' Alison said. She was beginning
to find the stew heavy going, but was determined not to
risk getting on the wrong side of Mrs Rumbold by failing
to clean her plate.

'Well, you take a jigger of brandy,' Mrs Rumbold said,
'and you add some Benedictine, just a little, then you
fill up with Advocaat. My Joe – that's Mr Rumbold – he
knows I really enjoy a brandy puff, so sometimes he'll
say, "Come along, we'll go along to the Good Intent
and give ourselves a treat," and that's what he knows
I'll ask for, though all he'll ever have is a pint of bitter
with a little gin in it. He's a very sober man, Joe, I'm
thankful to say. I'm a very lucky woman in more ways

than one. I've a good husband, a good home and a good job. All I wish is I'd had some children. You got any children, dear?'

'No,' Alison said.

'And is it true your husband's left you? That's what she said.'

Alison nodded without speaking.

'Ah well,' Mrs Rumbold said, 'you may be better off as you are. You never can tell. And you're young, you may always marry again if you haven't been put off it for good. All men aren't the same, remember. Some people say they are, but take it from me, that's just a manner of speaking.'

'Do you live near here?' Alison asked, wanting to get her off the subject of marriage.

'Only a mile or so up the road. I come on my bicycle.'

'Is there a village near?'

'Not what you'd call a village. There's the Good Intent and round the corner from it there's the Blue Boar and a bit further on there's the Green Man, all quite nice, but the Good Intent's the one I like. The Green Man's on the main road and it's mainly patronized by people passing through, and the Blue Boar's where people go for serious drinking, but the Good Intent's the friendly one where you go if you want to hear what's going on in the place. And there's a post office next door where you can buy things like beans and soups and toothpaste and all that. But you'll want to go into Helsington to do your proper shopping. I'll give you a list of places where Mrs Eckersall runs accounts.'

'She told me the place was very lonely,' Alison said. 'It doesn't sound it.'

'Well, that's what the other girls said, that the place was too lonely. I told Mrs Eckersall, I said, "You shouldn't get girls from London," I said, "they'll never settle down.

You want a Helsington girl." That Linda, the one who left last week, the moment I saw her I knew she wouldn't stay. Lazy, for one thing. Expected me to do half her work for her, like cleaning vegetables and all that. And the work here isn't heavy, mind, with them only down at the weekend. The other one, Sally, wasn't like that. She was a very good little worker and nice-natured. Pretty too. It really took me by surprise when she went off like she did. I've sometimes wondered, though mind you don't repeat it, if Mr Eckersall wasn't the trouble. I think he bothered the girl a bit and she wasn't the type to put up with it. Not like Linda. She'd have encouraged him. Not that he needs much encouragement, as you may find out for yourself. But you don't want to worry about it too much. Just slap him down good and hard if he tries anything on and you'll find he takes it in the right spirit. That poor little Sally, I don't think she understood that. Now what about some apple tart, dear?'

Alison had already eaten twice the amount she usually had for lunch but she said that apple tart sounded delicious. Unfortunately Mrs Rumbold's pastry was very solid.

Working at it stubbornly, Alison said, 'And both girls simply vanished without warning, did they?'

'Well, more or less,' Mrs Rumbold answered. 'Sally left Mrs Eckersall a letter. She went off one Thursday evening when no one was here and just left this letter behind her. Linda at least telephoned Mrs Eckersall that she was going. That was last Friday. I know it, I heard her. And it's my opinion she'd have stayed on if she'd had a boy-friend in Helsington. She spent a good many of her evenings in the Blue Boar, trying to pick one up, but the truth was, and I don't want you to think I'm being unkind, she wasn't all that attractive.'

'Did Sally have a boy-friend?' Alison asked.

'So it said.'

'What said?'

'The letter she left. She said she was going away with her boy-friend.'

'Did you ever meet him?'

'Well, no, I don't think I ever did. I mean, I thought I knew who her boy-friend was, but the one I thought it was is still around, so it can't have been him, can it?'

'Did you see the letter?'

But Alison knew that she was asking too many questions all of a sudden. She resolved that that should be the last for the moment.

Mrs Rumbold nodded. The heavy lids of her eyes drooped even lower over them as she frowned at her plate.

'I shouldn't have done it, but I found it lying open on Mrs Eckersall's dressing-table and my curiosity got the better of me and I read it. But I don't want you to think I make a rule of doing that kind of thing and I told the police about it when they came. I like to be open and above-board with everyone.'

'The *police*?' Alison said. Then she felt that she had overdone her surprise, that it sounded very over-acted.

But Mrs Rumbold continued to study her plate and to wrestle, glowering, with her uneasy conscience.

'Yes, her family put them on to it,' she said. 'First her brother came down, Mr Burnaby, asking what had become of her and when we'd heard of her last. Seems he tried telephoning her several times and she never answered and he'd heard nothing of her for a week or two and he was worried. She hadn't gone home when she left here and she hadn't let any of her family know what she was doing. She hadn't said anything to them about the boy-friend. Of course we couldn't tell him anything about that, not knowing any more than he did, so he went to the police and they came, asking questions, and it turned out it was lucky I'd read the letter, though I was ever so embarrassed having to admit it, because I was able to tell them the same as Mrs Eckersall about what was in it. She hadn't kept the letter, you see, she'd just thrown it away. And the police asked if Sally had taken all her belongings with her, which she had, and they asked what we knew about the boy-friend and all that. And I'm sure I don't know if they've ever found out anything about who he was or where they went, but if they did they'll have told her family, I suppose. I'm sure I hope so. She was a nice little thing.'

Alison broke her resolution to ask no more questions. 'What did Mrs Eckersall say when she found you'd read the letter? Was she angry?'

'Well, it was kind of funny,' Mrs Rumbold said. 'But she often is. You never know how she'll take things. She gave me one of those sort of hard looks of hers and I thought, "Here we go, I'm in for it," and then all she said was, "Don't worry, Mrs Rumbold, most of us read other people's letters when we get the chance, even if we don't admit it, just like we listen at doors. I always listen at doors when I can," she said, "so I know ever so much more than a lot of people think I do." Then she gave a queer sort of laugh which kind of gave me the shivers and went out and that's all she ever said about it. Now shall I make you some coffee, dear, or would you like to go off and have a rest? I'll just pop these things in the dishwasher, then I'll be off home. Like I said, there's nothing for you to do today but get your own supper and there's plenty for that in the fridge. If I was you I'd take it easy this afternoon, then tomorrow I'll tell you where to go to do the shopping and what kind of things they like and all that.'

Alison thanked her for all her kindness and said that perhaps she would make herself some tea later but that now she would take Mrs Rumbold's advice and lie down.

She had no intention of lying down. What she wanted as soon as she was alone was to prowl through the house unobserved. She helped Mrs Rumbold stack the things that they had used in the dishwasher and went up to her room, and presently, watching from the window, saw Mrs Rumbold take her bicycle out of the garage and pedal away down the drive. Knowing now that the house was empty, Alison started to wander about in it.

Of course she did not know what she was looking for and apart from the fact that Mr and Mrs Eckersall slept in separate rooms, the only object of interest that she discovered was a walnut bureau in a small room on the ground floor that was furnished as a kind of office or study, and the bureau was only of interest because the top of it was locked.

Everything else in the house was open to her probing fingers, clothes cupboards, chests of drawers, a drinks cupboard, a pretty writing-table with its pigeonholes crammed with letters. She read some of the letters, but they were only the normal sort that accumulate in any household, bills and receipts and invitations. Just the walnut bureau was locked. But unfortunately picking locks was not one of Alison's skills, so leaving the bureau as it was and moving on to the french windows that led into the garden, she pushed them open and stepped outside.

Walking across the lawn to where Barry Jones was working on a long herbaceous border, she stood watching him for a moment, then said, 'You haven't always been a gardener, have you?'

He gave a start and turned. He had not heard her footsteps on the grass. Rubbing an earthy hand across his forehead, he answered, 'You haven't always been a cook.'

'No, but I've a good reason for wanting to be one now,' she said.

'Ah yes, the husband who walked out on you. I heard all about him from Mrs Rumbold. Where'd he go when he left you?'

'South America.'

'Read the newspapers, you get the idea a lot of people take off for South America,' he said. 'Anyway to countries we haven't got extradition treaties with.'

'You aren't married?'

'Not as of this time.'

'You mean you have been?'

'You do ask questions, don't you? Yes, I have been, but too long ago to remember. She walked out on me when my troubles began. I don't blame her. I expect I'd have done the same.'

'What were your troubles?'

'Haven't you heard? I'm a mental case. Any morning now I may wake up and think I'm God. It's a thing that happens to me from time to time.'

'What do you do when it happens?'

'I rule the world. You won't notice much difference in my actual behaviour, but I'll know that everything you do is at my bidding. I'm so powerful, you just wouldn't believe.'

'But you still haven't told me what you were before you took to gardening.'

He turned back to the flowerbed and began to hoe at some weeds round a clump of lupins. Alison thought that he was not going to answer her, but then he went on, 'I was a schoolmaster of a sort. I taught carpentry. It was just a miserable little school for witless kids. I hated the school and the boys and the other masters from the day I went there. I hate a lot of things. I'm told that's what's the matter with me. If I could learn to love my neighbour instead of hating the bastard and wanting to use my great power to kick him all the way down to hell, I'd be as right as rain. Funny thing though, it comes quite easily to me to love flowers. Grass too. I'm very fond of grass and green things generally. Is that all you want to know?'

'Have you told all this to the Eckersalls?'

'Since you ask me, I don't believe I told them anything about loving grass.' His tone was sardonic. 'They wouldn't have been as interested as you. All they wanted to know was would I clear up this garden for them. Love and hate didn't come into the conversation. But I told them I'd been barmy, if that's what's worrying you. Not much good trying to hide it, was there, when they spotted as fast as you did that I hadn't been a gardener all my life and must have reasons for wanting to be one now? So I told them I'd had a mental breakdown and had been recommended to do manual work for my health, as was perfectly true. And I might add that the last few weeks, when I've had the run of the garden and nobody bothering me, have been one of the best bits of my life.'

'I'm sorry if I've been bothering you,' Alison said. 'I only thought, since we're both going to be working here, we might as well get to know one another.'

'No bother,' he said. 'Very pleasant, as a matter of fact. You don't chatter. I shouldn't wonder if we'll get along. Just as long as you don't ask me too many of those questions. If ever you find yourself starting to wonder about me, just say to yourself, "The man's crazy about gardens." See that lawn? It's nearly all daisies. When I'm finished with it, it's going to be all grass. There won't be a weed in it. It'll be as near to velvet as those nice pink cheeks of yours. And d'you see those roses there? They're past saving. God knows when they were last pruned. They're coming out and I'll manure the ground and put fresh bushes in this autumn. If I'm still here, that is. And this border, it's only got ordinary stuff in it, nothing interesting . . .' He broke off with the first laugh that Alison had heard him give. 'You see, there's so much to think about and plan and work at, I just might manage to stay sane for a while.'

Under a layer of self-mockery there was a startling intensity in his voice. Alison wondered if he had been in a mental home recently and if that was why the freedom of the garden, with the independence in it that the Eckersalls plainly allowed him, meant so much to him.

'Well, good luck,' she said vaguely and wandered on, going a short walk round the garden, then returning to the house and spending the next hour or so in the kitchen, trying to memorize where the pots and pans were kept and finding what there was in the refrigerator and making plans for the meals for the weekend.

She wondered if she would find herself hopelessly inadequate when it came to doing the job for which she was going to be paid. Not that that mattered to her very much. It was not going to take her long to find out if there was any point at all in her staying. But pride was involved. She wanted to do the job well.

Presently she boiled herself an egg, made some toast and coffee and went upstairs to her room.

What there was about it she could not have said, but once she had settled down in it she was overcome by an appalling sense of desolation. She had not felt it in the rest of the house and garden, but in this little room which was to be her home for the present she felt horrifyingly alone. In spite of the chintz and the patchwork quilt and some flower prints on the walls, it felt as impersonal as any room in a hotel. It was difficult to believe that anyone had ever stayed here for more than a night or two.

It was as if the people who had been in it before her had had all signs of their existence blotted out.

She realized that this had nothing to do with the room, but was all in her own mind. The fact that in the empty drawers and cupboards not a forgotten packet of tissues remained, not even a safety pin, was simply a result of Mrs Rumbold's efficiency. There was no reason to find it in any way disturbing. Yet it seemed extraordinarily chilling. She gave a sudden shiver and turned to her photograph of Mark.

As she had caught herself doing sometimes recently, she tried talking to it. She kept her voice to a whisper, because although she knew that she had the house to herself, she felt as if there might be presences in the house that could overhear her. But the photograph seemed less responsive than usual. She could only sense reproof in the eyes that looked so directly at her and followed her about the room. It made her feel almost angry with him. For if only she had been able to form even the most illusory contact with him, it was possible, she thought, that she might have been given some hint as to what she should do next. But the little room felt utterly empty. It seemed even to drain her of her own identity so that she felt almost unsure of her actual presence there. Presently she began to yawn and went to bed early.

But that was a mistake. As soon as she lay down she felt wide awake. She had not really been expecting to be able to sleep, for she was never very good at sleeping in strange beds and besides that she had too many disturbing thoughts on her mind for sleep to come easily. But she was not prepared for the sense of extreme tension that took hold of her as soon as she turned out the light. It was both mental and physical and was not exactly fear and not a simple nervous restlessness either. After a while she could stand it no longer. She got up, put on her dressing-gown and slippers and went out into the passage, meaning to make herself some tea.

She was half-way down the stairs when the front-door bell rang.

There was a grandfather clock facing her in the hall and she noticed that the time was a quarter to one.

An odd time to come visiting. She did not know what to do. Standing still, she listened. After a moment the bell rang again, a long, impatient ring, and she thought that she heard voices outside. Women's voices. It was the fact that they were women's that made her bold enough to go down the stairs and unlock the door. But as she did so her glance went towards an old-fashioned brass umbrella stand in which she noticed thankfully a walking stick with a heavy, bone-handled crook. She would be able to snatch it, she thought, if it turned out that she needed it. Opening the door a few inches, she looked out.

In the porch stood two small women. They were so alike that they could only have been twins, though one was two or three inches taller than the other. The smaller one stood slightly behind her sister, their shoulders almost touching. Later Alison was to discover that this was how they always walked about, giving the impression that the taller one was leading the smaller one along like a child. They looked about sixty. Both wore grey knitted pixie hoods which framed their small clay-coloured faces and completely hid their hair. They wore tweed coats, slightly different in colour though identical in cut, thick stockings and old suede shoes in which it was evident that they did their gardening, for they were heavily caked with earth.

'We do beg your pardon if we've disturbed you,' the taller one said in a soft, rustling little voice, 'but we saw a light go on upstairs so we knew someone must be awake.

Of course we stay up to all hours ourselves because there are so many interesting things to be seen in the dark. And seeing your light, we thought we'd come over and ask you if we could borrow some treacle.'

She paused, suddenly thrusting her head forward and peering at Alison as if she had only just noticed that she was a stranger.

'Oh dear, I don't think we've ever met before,' the little woman went on. 'The people here, they come and go so often, it's sometimes difficult to remember. I'm very sorry if we startled you. The Eckersalls are used to us, of course. Our name is Fisk. We live next door. And we meant to buy some treacle when we went to the grocer in Helsington this morning, but we completely forgot it, so we thought that just perhaps – but we don't want to be a nuisance – you might be able to help us out.'

How you could possibly be more of a nuisance than by rousing your neighbours at a quarter to one in the morning to borrow some treacle Alison could not imagine.

However, she replied, 'I don't really know if there's any treacle in the house. I'm quite new here. But if you don't mind waiting a moment, I'll go and see.'

'How kind,' both sisters said in their hushed little voices. 'How very kind.'

'Because, you see,' the taller one went on, 'it's really very important.'

Alison left them in the porch and went to the kitchen. In the store cupboard she found a half-pound tin of Golden Syrup. She went back with it to the door.

'Is this any use?' she asked. 'It's all I can find.'

'Oh dear, oh dear,' the taller sister said tragically, 'we need seven pounds.'

'At least,' the smaller one said.

'Then I'm awfully sorry, I can't help.'

'Of course, it's all our own fault,' the taller one con-

tinued, 'forgetting it this morning. Now we'll have to wait
till tomorrow and hope nothing dreadful happens in the
meantime. You see, there's a thrush's nest in that lovely
wild rose by your garage and the eggs are going to hatch
any time now and that dreadful Colonel Mayberry from
down the road will be after the babies like a streak of
lightning and gobble them up, the monster.'

'Oh yes, we've seen him prowling around already,' her
sister said. 'He knows there's a nest there. And he's much
too fat as it is. He doesn't need poor little birds to feed
on.'

They made it sound like cannibalism. Alison was glad
when the taller one explained, 'Of course, that isn't his
real name, you know. We don't actually know what it is,
but he belongs to Colonel Mayberry, who's an excellent
man – oh yes, quite excellent, but as we've told him, he
ought to control that creature of his better. A great big
ginger tom.'

'But what are you going to do with the treacle?' Alison
asked.

'Ah, that's a tip your nice gardener gave us. "Spread
treacle on the ground all round the bush," he said, "and
the cat won't go near it. They don't like getting their
paws sticky." Such a very practical idea and obvious, of
course, once you've thought of it. So that's what we
decided we'd do. And then, of all foolish things, we forgot
to buy the treacle. Well, I do hope we haven't disturbed
you too much, dropping in, and we'll tell you how it
works – the treacle, I mean – because I'm sure you'll be
interested. And if you see a horrid big ginger tom, do
chase him away. Good evening, Miss . . . ?'

'Mrs Goodrich.'

'Good evening, Mrs Goodrich.'

The two little women, whose pointed pixie hoods made
them look like witches in the shadows, turned, keeping very

close to one another, and stole softly away into the darkness.

Witches were something that Alison could cope with. Her talk with them had cured her of her need for a hot drink. She went back to bed and was asleep almost instantly.

CHAPTER III

BY THE TIME that Mrs Rumbold arrived next morning on her bicycle Alison had finished her breakfast and was sitting at the kitchen table, making a list of the things that she thought would be needed for the weekend.

She told Mrs Rumbold of her visitors of the night before and of their need for treacle at a quarter to one in the morning.

Mrs Rumbold giggled, kicked off the rather high-heeled shoes in which she had arrived and slipped on her red velvet bedroom slippers, which apparently had a home in one of the kitchen cupboards.

'That's nothing for them,' she said. Her big fleshy face was flushed from her recent exercise. 'You don't want to worry about them. They've been there as long as anyone can remember and they're quite harmless. Miss Wendy and Miss Kitty. It's Miss Wendy does most of the talking because Miss Kitty's just a bit wanting. Not that Miss Wendy is exactly what you'd call normal, but she's a bit sharper like than her sister. But they're ever so kind and it's just like them to worry about Colonel Mayberry's cat getting at a bird's nest. Now I'm going upstairs to make up the beds and do the bedrooms. Is there anything I can tell you before I go?'

'Can you tell me the kind of thing I ought to cook for dinner?' Alison asked. 'Mrs Eckersall told me they like plain food, but that can mean anything from sausages up to *coq au vin*.'

Mrs Rumbold had gone into the passage and was extracting a vacuum cleaner from a cupboard there.

'You'd be safe giving them fillet steaks and salad,' she

said, 'and perhaps an avocado first, if you can find a nice ripe one, or else some smoked salmon. You can get the real stuff, not frozen, from Green and Buckley's in the High Street. And no sweet, just cheese, because they worry about their figures. When they say simple, of course, they don't mean cheap. You needn't ever worry about spending their money for them. And you needn't worry about drinks, because Mr Eckersall will look after that. Or if you can't get nice fillet steaks, you could get some veal from Hamilton's, just across the way from Green and Buckley's. They nearly always have veal on a Friday.'

She went on with her instructions while she took her dusters and polish out of the cupboard, telling Alison where the various shops were at which the Eckersalls ran accounts and that the only serious problem she would have to face were that Mr Eckersall refused to eat onions, while Mrs Eckersall never touched a potato. She was just setting off for the stairs when the telephone rang.

'You'd better answer that,' she said. 'It's probably her wanting to know if you got here safely. Anyway, I'm no good on the telephone. I can never understand what anyone says.'

She strode off with her paraphernalia while the ringing went on.

There were several extensions, including one in the kitchen. Alison lifted the one there and recited the number written on the dial.

'Mrs Goodrich?' The voice with the faint rasp in it was easy to recognize. 'I'm going to call you Alison, do you mind? Have you settled in? Is everything all right? I just rang up to say we're bringing June Pullen down with us for the weekend. My husband's secretary. And that means three for dinner and Mrs Rumbold will have to get her room ready for her. She always has the room

opposite the top of the stairs. Mrs Rumbold will know.
How are you getting on with her? You won't get across
her on any account, will you, because she's an absolute
treasure and I don't know what I'd do without her.'

Her questions tumbled out one after the other, giving
Alison no time to answer any of them. As soon as she
began to say that all was well between her and Mrs
Rumbold, Mrs Eckersall said that that was fine and rang
off.

Alison returned to the list that she had left on the kitchen
table and began altering all the quantities that she had
written down, since there would be an extra person to feed,
then went upstairs and above the roar of the vacuum
cleaner in Mrs Eckersall's bedroom, said to Mrs Rumbold,
'You were right, it was Mrs Eckersall and she said they're
bringing a Miss Pullen down for the weekend.'

Mrs Rumbold pressed the switch of the vacuum cleaner
and the sound died.

'What's that?'

Alison repeated what she had said.

'Well!' Mrs Rumbold exclaimed and a heavy frown
made thick creases across her forehead. Alison thought
that she was annoyed at having to prepare an extra room,
but when she offered to do it for her Mrs Rumbold gave
a toss of her head and repeated, 'Well!' Something
sparkled in her inquisitive little eyes. 'Is that woman blind
or is it she doesn't care? I've taken to wondering about
that lately. At first I took for granted they'd pulled the
wool over her eyes and she just hadn't an idea what was
going on, but she isn't a fool, would you say? Mrs
Eckersall isn't a fool, don't you agree with me?'

Alison hesitated. The truth was that she had not begun
to make up her mind what Mrs Eckersall was, fool or
wise, good, bad or just deeply indifferent to nearly
everything.

'Of course she isn't,' Mrs Rumbold said impatiently. 'She's got eyes, same as you and me. And if she can't see what her husband and that girl are up to here in her own house, then, I'm beginning to think, it's because she's decided not to see. How she can do it I don't know. I never could, could you? Unless, of course, she thinks if she holds out she'll get him back, as she will, I shouldn't wonder, only there'll be another after the Pullen girl, and another after her and so on until he's past the age for it. That's the only thing that'll ever cure him. He's no good, that man, though polite, mind you, and quite considerate in his way. But if I was his wife I'd give him his marching papers.'

'What's his job?' Alison asked. 'Or hasn't he got one?'

'He's chairman of a firm called Longthorpe Pricket International Appointments Ltd., or something like that. Finds jobs for people who want to go abroad, that sort of thing. Classy jobs, you know. There seems to be plenty of money in it.'

'Perhaps that's what Mrs Eckersall wants most,' Alison suggested.

'Not her, and you won't think so either when you know her a bit better. She's very warm-hearted really. Got strong feelings. Same as you, I shouldn't wonder, keeping your husband's photo on your dressing-table even when he's left you. That is your husband, I suppose?'

So she had already been into Alison's room to have a look round.

'Yes,' Alison said.

Mrs Rumbold picked up a duster and began vigorously polishing the mahogany bedhead.

'Very good-looking,' she said. 'Looks a reliable sort of chap too. I can understand your feeling for him. I might care about someone like that myself. And you still hope he'll come back, don't you? Ah well, perhaps he will.

I can't really understand it, wanting a man back who's treated you like that, but we're all different, which is a good thing, so they say. Now you go and do your shopping and I'll get the Pullen girl's room ready for her, and I know it isn't my business what they get up to, so don't stand there staring as if I'd said something shocking about them.' She paused. 'It isn't what I said about your husband you mind, is it, dear? I didn't mean to hurt you.'

'No, that's all right,' Alison said. 'Where do they keep the car keys?'

Mrs Rumbold told her and Alison went downstairs, found a large shopping basket in the kitchen and went out to the garage.

Driving into the town she saw that there had been heavy rain during the night. Trees and hedges had a shiny, fresh-washed look and there were glittering puddles on the road. Because the morning was fine the shining sky that they reflected made them look like tatters of blue silk on the greasy grey of the roadway.

For some reason she was in a better mood than she had been in for the last twenty-four hours. She was less apprehensive than she had been the day before and in a way had begun to look forward to the evening when the Eckersalls were due to arrive. Probably it was because she had something positive to do now. She had always found it easy to become immersed in shopping and cooking. Also she was curious to see June Pullen. She had a feeling that between them this girl and the Eckersalls might unintentionally reveal something that would be useful to her. If the situation between them was really as Mrs Rumbold had described it, then there must be tension, and tension has a way of making people reveal themselves far more than they intend.

Alison found the car park to which Mrs Rumbold had directed her and emerged from it, carrying the basket, into a street of shops. She found Hamilton's, the butcher, quite soon and bought the fillet steaks that Mrs Rumbold had suggested. Then she went looking for Green and Buckley's, which turned out to be one of those big, old-fashioned grocers, now almost extinct, fragrant with the aroma of coffee, cheeses, herbs and spices, where shop assistants in long white aprons bow to you over counters and ask how they can serve you. Alison began buying recklessly for the sheer pleasure of talking to one of these dignified men and it was only the way that her basket was beginning to bulge that stopped her. She had her purchases put on Mrs Eckersall's account and staggered out into the street.

As she reached it someone on the other side of it called out, 'Sally!'

She stood still, her heart pounding violently.

She was not sure where the cry had come from. There was a knot of people standing by some traffic lights, waiting to cross the street, and the cry could have come from any of them. She stayed where she was, taut with excitement, waiting for the lights to change.

Before they did a young man shot out of the group, plunged in front of a lorry and a taxi, the drivers of which both cursed him, reached the pavement near to where Alison was standing and called again, 'Sally!'

Alison waited for him. He thrust his way between some strolling shoppers and grasped her by the arm. He was of medium height and stockily built, with a round, pleasant face with smooth cheeks, blue eyes, a blunt nose, a wide, friendly mouth and fair, curly hair. He looked agreeable and ordinary and did not seem in any way remarkable except for the strange way, as he and Alison looked at one another, that the healthy colour of his face drained away, leaving it a dull, chalky white.

'I'm sorry – mistake – took you for someone else.

Extraordinary resemblance. I do apologize if I startled
you. Very sorry.'

Letting go of her arm so abruptly that it felt almost as
if he were throwing it back at her, he turned and shot
off down the street.

'Wait!' she called after him. 'Wait!'

She thought that he heard her, for he half turned his
head, but he did not pause.

With her heavy basket on her arm she could not run
after him. In a moment he had turned a corner and was
out of sight.

She was still standing there, wondering how she could
possibly find him again, when she felt another hand take
hold of her arm. It was not a firm grip this time, as the
young man's had been, but rather a little tweak at her
sleeve. She started violently, then turned and saw Miss
Wendy Fisk at her elbow. Her sister stood close behind
her.

'We've got our treacle!' Miss Wendy said triumphantly.
'We thought you'd like to know. And we've got two nice
paintbrushes too and we're going to start painting the
treacle round the bush as soon as we can. It'll be such
fun and it'll put paid to that horrid Colonel Mayberry.
We'll have to come over to your side of the fence, I'm
afraid, but we've promised Mr Jones we won't get it on
the steps of his flat. And you'll come and see our dear little
birds when they hatch, won't you? Now come along,
Kitty, we mustn't keep Mrs Goodrich. We can see she's
busy.'

They walked away, carrying what looked like a large
can of paint between them, but which was presumably
the treacle.

Alison finished her shopping and made her way back
to the car park. When she had stowed the basket in the
car there was still one important thing that she wanted

to do before returning to the Eckersalls' house. She went looking for a telephone and found one in a post office not far from Green and Buckley's. Going into the booth, she dialled the number of Geoffrey's office.

When she got through to him he immediately started asking questions, which she interrupted impatiently, 'Yes, yes, I've settled in and the family are arriving this evening. I'm in Helsington at the moment, doing the shopping. But I've just had a rather curious experience. I don't know what to make of it. I've been mistaken for Sally.'

She described to Geoffrey the young man who had rushed up to her and rushed away again.

'Odd,' Geoffrey said. 'There's really not the slightest resemblance between you.'

'There may be that thing people call a family resemblance that none of the family can ever see,' she said. 'The trouble is, I haven't the faintest idea who he is or how to find out about him.'

'And that's the only thing of interest that's happened so far?'

'Except that Mrs Rumbold's been dropping dark hints about Mr Eckersall's ways with women. And if he's really as bad as she says, I suppose it just might have made Sally pack up and go, only that doesn't explain why we've heard nothing from her. There's been some talk about that letter she left behind about the mysterious boy-friend she was going away with, but as we agreed, that doesn't sound like Sally. The first thing she's generally done with any new boy-friend has been to take him the round of the family.'

'Perhaps she found one who had reasons for not wanting to meet her family. That's the letter I heard about, of course, when I saw the Eckersalls, but I didn't feel sure it ever existed.'

'I think it did. Mrs Rumbold confessed to me she'd found

it and read it and she was embarrassed enough about having done it to convince me she really had.'

'And the family arrives today?'

'Yes. Meanwhile I've got the gardener for company. He's already told me about his mental breakdown.'

'Well, watch your step. Remember Katrina and I are anxious about you.'

'What's worrying me is that I'm very doubtful if there's anything here to be anxious about. I think I'd be feeling happier if there were a smell of something sinister. I'd feel less helpless. I don't see how anything I'm doing is going to help us find Sally. However, perhaps I'll have more to tell you after the weekend. It may help if I can find out who this man is who mistook me for her.'

They said goodbye to one another and rang off. Alison returned to the car and drove it back to the house.

By the time that she arrived Mrs Rumbold had already left for home. Alison unpacked her basket, then settled down at the kitchen table with some bread and cheese and afterwards made some coffee. She was at the sink, rinsing the crockery that she had used, when she heard a ring at the front-door bell.

She was not expecting the young woman who stood in the porch. Yet perhaps if she had paid more attention when they had met before to the kind of person that the young woman was, she would have done so.

'Oh,' she said, 'it's you.'

Linda Prentice nodded and as Alison said nothing more and did not move, asked, 'Aren't you going to ask me in? I know there's no one here but you and I can smell coffee. I could do with a cup of coffee. I had a cup on the train, with a sandwich, but you know what muck they give you.'

'The coffee's finished,' Alison said.

She still did not move. Her mind was working slowly. She would have liked to have had some inkling of what had brought Linda Prentice here before she let her into the house. She felt a conviction that there was something menacing in her presence.

There was nothing notably menacing in her appearance, even if, as Mrs Rumbold had said, she was not attractive. She had a stocky figure with thick legs and short, broad feet on which she looked planted in the porch almost as if she intended to take root there and start growing. She had a round, white, dimpled face, rather doughy in texture, with eyes of a very pale grey with scanty lashes. Her mouth, when she spoke, had a trick of opening into a rectangle which showed good teeth and a good deal of pale gum. Her hair was bleached to a harsh yellow. Green eye-shadow outlined her eyes and her lipstick was of the same scarlet as the suit she was wearing. She had on white lacey gloves and was carrying a big white plastic handbag.

'Well, you needn't look so afraid of me,' she said, her voice thin and mocking. 'All I've asked for is a cup of coffee.'

'So far,' Alison said.

'Well, yes. It's just that I've been doing some thinking since you got me to meet you in London and I think you and I ought to have a talk. Of course I can go ahead standing here, if that's what you want, but that Barry may come out into the garden at any time and for all I know might take it into his head to come and see what's going on. And I've got a feeling you'd sooner keep our talk private.'

She smiled her rectangular smile. She was threatening her, Alison realized, though she was not yet sure in what way. But her first impression that there was something menacing about the girl had certainly been correct.

Unwillingly she stood aside and let her in.

Linda Prentice walked straight to the drawing-room,

chose the most comfortable chair and dropped into it.

'Might as well make ourselves at home since there's no one else about,' she said. 'Now what about a drink, if there's no coffee? That's what I'd really like, a whisky. I took a bus from the station and the bus stop's a good half mile away. I've had quite a walk.'

'I'll make some more coffee,' Alison said and went back to the kitchen.

When she returned with a new jug of coffee and cups and saucers on a tray, she found that Linda Prentice was standing at the window, looking out at Barry Jones, who had appeared in the garden and was wandering about in it, picking flowers.

Alison poured out the coffee and said, 'Here you are.'

Linda did not turn.

'What d'you make of that man?' she asked. 'Like him, do you?'

'He seems quite inoffensive,' Alison answered.

'That's what I thought at first.'

'What happened then?'

'Well, haven't they told you he's mad? Of course he's very cunning at hiding it. They all are, you know, ever so cunning. The mad, I mean. But once you know, you'll find there are all sorts of little ways he gives himself away.'

'Your coffee'll get cold,' Alison said.

Linda turned back from the window and picked up her cup.

'I don't mind telling you now,' she said, 'he was one of the reasons I didn't mind giving up my job here when you phoned and suggested it. I didn't like the way he looked at me. He's got a kind of a cruel stare, d'you know what I mean? I was really afraid of him by the time I left.'

'I haven't heard anyone else say anything of the same sort,' Alison said.

Linda gave a little smirk of a smile. 'Could be he's only like that if he fancies you. A kind of a pervert. But he isn't what I came here to talk about.'

'I didn't think he was.'

'Well, do let's sit down and be comfortable.' Linda settled herself in the same chair as before and sipped her coffee. 'You're looking at me as if I'd come here to make trouble for you. I haven't, honestly. I just want a friendly chat.'

Alison sat down in a chair facing her. 'Could it be about money?'

Linda laughed. 'Now how did you guess that? Yes, I've been thinking, if you were ready to give me fifty pounds to leave my job here so that you could get it, you must have a pretty good reason for wanting to come. I don't know what it is and I don't mind not knowing. I'm not trying to pry. What you're up to is your own business and I'm not inquisitive. But fifty pounds doesn't go far these days and here I am, out of a job because I was ready to oblige you. So, as I said, I've been thinking – '

'How much?' Alison interrupted.

'Now don't be like that,' Linda said. 'I'm sure you can understand my point of view. I know this job's important to you for some reason or other and I know if I went to Mrs Eckersall and told her you'd paid me fifty pounds to get out of it, she'd have you out pretty fast. So asking for another fifty doesn't seem to me unreasonable. Not greedy. And I really do need the money.'

Alison drank some coffee. She had never been black-mailed before and she found herself for the moment more interested in the situation and her own reaction to it than merely scared or angry. Without any emotion to speak of she watched herself sipping her coffee and regarding the girl and thinking about the problem that she had had flung at her.

It would have been different, she realized, if Linda had been able to frighten her, but although it would be annoying and frustrating to lose her job, Alison would not suffer any terrible dread of exposure. All the same, Linda had a small degree of power over her and she recognized that she must make up her mind quickly what she was going to do about it.

She had gone on gazing at Linda while these thoughts went through her mind and suddenly Linda exploded, 'Don't look at me like that, as if I was dirt! You'd do the same in my place.'

'I'm sure you find it cheering to think so,' Alison said. 'You say you want fifty pounds.'

'Yes,' Linda said sullenly. 'What you gave me before wasn't enough for giving up a good job.'

'In spite of the cruel stare of the mad gardener?'

'What? Oh, him. I could have managed him if I'd had to.'

'But you were glad to get away from him, all the same.'

'That won't stop me going to Mrs Eckersall and telling her how you paid me to leave. The question is, do I get that fifty?'

Alison supposed that she could have bargained, but that was something at which she had never had much practice.

'All right, I'll give you a cheque,' she said. 'But let me make it clear to you, it won't work a second time. I'm not expecting to be here very long, so if you come again you may not find me.'

She got up to fetch her handbag, which had her cheque-book in it.

In the doorway of the drawing-room she was stopped by Barry Jones, who was just coming in, carrying a big armful of flowers.

'I brought these for the house,' he said. 'Mrs Eckersall

always likes to have plenty . . .' He broke off, seeing Linda Prentice.

'Hallo, Barry,' she said demurely. There was a teasing note in her voice, as if she enjoyed being able to provoke the scowl with which he regarded her. 'Lovely flowers you've got there. Are you still as fond of flowers as ever?'

He looked suspiciously at Alison. 'Do you two know one another?'

'The acquaintance is superficial,' Alison said.

'When did you meet?'

'Now isn't that our own affair?' Linda said with a heavy kind of roguishness. 'As a matter of fact, we're old friends, and I got Alison the job when I left, and I thought I'd just like to drop in to see how she was getting along.'

'Because, I suppose, you just happened to be in the neighbourhood,' he said ironically. 'There's something here I don't understand and don't like.'

Alison then saw what Linda had meant by his cruel stare. She would not much have liked to have his slanting, greenish eyes give her the look that he gave Linda. When he looked back at Alison his face merely had its closed look. She did not like it much better than the other, but at least there was no open enmity in it.

He looked down at his armful of flowers.

'I'll put these in the kitchen,' he said. 'Mrs Eckersall likes them everywhere, including the bedrooms. Miss Pullen's too, don't forget.'

He ignored Linda as he left the room.

'There, didn't I tell you?' she exclaimed. 'But you like him, don't you, or you're sorry for him? I could tell from the way you looked at him. I suppose the two of you aren't up to something together, are you? That's a thought! Perhaps I ought to have asked for more than just fifty.'

'You wouldn't have got it,' Alison said. 'Wait here now and I'll get my cheque-book.'

'But if I told Mrs Eckersall you and Barry knew each other before you came here – '

'We didn't, so it wouldn't get you anywhere.'

'All right, all right, I was only joking. Fifty will do very nicely.'

Alison left her and went to the kitchen, where she had left her handbag.

The flowers that Barry had picked were in the sink. There were bunches of lilac and tulips and irises. Alison picked up her handbag, returned to the drawing-room with it, wrote out a cheque for fifty pounds and gave it to Linda. It was a relief that once she had it she had no desire to linger.

When she had gone Alison started arranging the flowers. She was no expert at it. She had no gift for making the single flower stand up in the one perfect position. The effects she achieved were generally of a slightly top-heavy luxuriance. But she enjoyed doing it, putting two vases in the drawing-room, a bowl in the middle of the dining-room table, and then taking three vases upstairs, one for each of the Eckersalls' bedrooms and the third for June Pullen's.

She was in June Pullen's bedroom, looking round for the best place for the vase, when something caught her eye through the window. The secretary's room, like Alison's, faced towards the road and what she saw was a man standing in the gateway, looking up at the house. There was an old white Volkswagen in the road behind him. He was a little too far away for her to be absolutely sure who he was, but his stocky build, his round face and ruffled fair hair made her almost certain that he was the young man who had mistaken her for Sally that morning in Helsington.

She went running down the stairs and out along the drive. But though she called out to him as she saw him get

into the car, by the time that she reached the gate he had
driven away.

Barry Jones, who was back at work on the herbaceous
border, looked round at her and said, 'Another old friend
of yours?'

CHAPTER IV

'Do you know who he is?' she asked.

Barry leant on his hoe, looking her over with one of his quizzical glances. 'Don't you?'

'No, I . . .' She paused. She had almost told him what had happened in Helsington that morning. But that was something, she knew, which it was essential that she should keep to herself.

'You seemed keen enough to talk to him,' he went on.

'I thought perhaps he might want to sell me an encyclopaedia,' she said. 'There's nothing I want quite as much as an encyclopaedia.'

'Ah, I know that feeling,' he said. 'But if you feel you've simply got to talk to somebody, even someone selling an encyclopaedia, if you're really as hard put to it as that, why not try me? I'm here. I speak English.'

'You don't like being talked to,' she said.

'Depends who by.'

'Well, tell me, have you ever seen that man before?'

He seemed to think the matter over carefully. But she did not feel that he was thinking of it at all. He was thinking about something, it might even have been about her rather than her interest in the stranger, but she was not surprised when he shrugged his shoulders.

'Can't say I remember it,' he said.

'He hasn't been to the house before?'

'Not while I've been around. And perhaps it was seeing me just now that frightened him off. Do you really not know him?'

Alison shook her head.

'And you want to?'

'I'd like to know who he is. The fact is,' she said, having decided on a half truth, 'I think he's a man who spoke to me in Helsington this morning and he seems to have followed me out here and I don't much like the feeling. I expect you're right that it was seeing you that scared him off, but suppose you aren't around next time.'

The corners of his mouth, under the drooping moustache, lifted slightly.

'If I'm not, you needn't come rushing down the drive, calling to him to stay. You can lock and bolt the doors against him.' He began hoeing again. 'I'd guess the simplest thing to do would be to ask Mrs Rumbold. If he's ever been around while she was here, she'll know all about him. She knows everyone in the place and everything that goes on.'

'That's a very sensible idea,' Alison said. 'I'll do that.'

'Sensible?' He slashed at some groundsel. 'I'm not sure if I can afford to be thought sensible. Let an idea like that get around and they'll send me back to teaching horrible little boys in some horrible little school. And I'd lose my, oh, so wonderful hold on reality again.'

'You know no one can make you do anything like that if you don't want to,' she said.

'Ah, you don't know what people can do to you once they've made up their minds. It can be almost as bad as what I want to do to them. And I'm not going to start telling a nice girl like you about things like that.'

She felt herself give an odd little shiver. She thought of Linda Prentice saying that the mad may be immensely cunning in concealing their condition, but that once you have become aware of it, there are all kinds of little ways in which they give themselves away. But what had suddenly shocked Alison was the realization that the converse can also be true. There are all sorts of little ways in which the sane give themselves away.

If Barry Jones had ever been mad in his life, she thought, if he had ever had such a thing as a mental breakdown, he would not have kept referring to it so continuously and in that cheerfully sardonic way. She had known one or two people who had really been down into the depths, suffering their terrors and their mysterious glories, and their attitudes to their experiences had been either secretiveness and shame or else a kind of exaltation. A rough sort of humour had not been at all characteristic of them.

To recognize this was the first really frightening thing that had happened to Alison since she had come to the Eckersalls' house. Why should a perfectly sane man keep trying to impress on others that he was mentally abnormal? Perhaps even dangerously abnormal?

Brooding on this, she strolled back to the house. She went to the kitchen and began to prepare the salad for dinner, washing the lettuce, salting the cucumber. With only fillet steaks to cook, she had not much else to do but to lay the table in the dining-room. Mrs Rumbold had told her what silver and china to put out. As she finished the table and was just thinking that the bowl of flowers that she had put in the middle of it looked very attractive, she heard the front door open and voices in the hall.

Her employers had arrived.

She went to the dining-room door, but Mrs Eckersall had gone straight to the kitchen, looking for her, and it was with Mr Eckersall that Alison came face to face.

She did not know what she had expected him to be like after all that Mrs Rumbold had told her about him, but it had not been anything like the man she saw. He was perhaps forty-five, of medium height, a little stout, with pale, clear skin and the beginnings of soft jowls under a rounded chin with a deep cleft in it. He had thick dark hair growing low in a widow's peak and soft, brown, friendly eyes. He was wearing a grey suede jacket, grey trousers and a grey and white striped shirt with a startling tie that looked like an imaginative portrayal of underwater life, all sea anemones, waving fronds of seaweed and little fishes.

Smiling, he held out his hand and as Alison took it remarked, 'My secretary chooses my ties. Please don't feel embarrassed, but I saw you look straight at it and blench. Everyone does. It's a look I've got to know. It's I who ought to feel embarrassed. But of course, flaunting something like this gives me time to arrange my face before anyone takes a good look at me. I can shed that look of worry and gloom that comes naturally to anyone who calls himself an executive nowadays, and become that cheery chap that everyone's delighted to have around because there can't be much wrong with the world if he can look so pleased with it. I do look pleased, don't I, Mrs Goodrich? I look a happy man?'

'Oh, Denis,' the girl who was standing behind him said, 'give the poor girl a little time to get used to you. And you might at least introduce me. I'm June Pullen, Mrs Goodrich, the secretary who chose the tie.'

She came forward and also shook hands with Alison.

She was about twenty-five, small, slender, almost bony, with a small, bright face surrounded by a tangle of brown curls. She was wearing tight jeans and a sloppy sweater which showed every line of her immature-looking body.

'But I *am* a happy man,' Mr Eckersall said. 'I want to make that clear. I've an adoring wife, a devoted secretary – yes, my darling, you are devoted, even if your taste is appalling – I've a charming country house and now I've a beautiful housekeeper too. Where did Louise find you, Mrs Goodrich? I know she has a genius for that kind of thing. For all kinds of things. For anything you could

name. But this time she's surpassed herself. How did she
discover you?'

'She discovered us,' Mrs Eckersall said, returning from
the kitchen. 'Literally came to us and asked us to employ
her.'

She had shoes on today, which made her taller than her
husband. Her pale gold hair, which had been piled high
on her head when Alison had seen her last, tumbled
loosely about her shoulders. She was in a casual-looking
camel-coloured trouser suit. Except that she was still
wearing the flashing diamond on her finger, she was dis-
concertingly unlike Alison's memory of her.

She went on, 'How are you, Alison? Have you settled
in all right? Run into any problems?'

'Not so far,' Alison said.

'But of course you won't stay long,' Mrs Eckersall ran
on. 'We both understood that, didn't we, when we talked
before? But at least we did understand it. We know where
we are. And you aren't going to vanish suddenly like the
other two, are you? You'll give us reasonable warning,
is that agreed?'

'Ah, you can see she's reasonable,' Mr Eckersall said.
'Very well balanced, very well adjusted. But the odd thing
is, Mrs Goodrich, I feel we've met before. Haven't we
sometime?'

Alison smiled and shook her head.

'But I feel sure of it,' he said.

'You've no need to say that,' his wife said. 'You aren't
trying to make a pick-up in a pub.'

'Which is why you can assume I mean what I say,' he
retorted. He smiled, but his voice was suddenly acid.

Alison's impulse was to get away from the hall as fast
as she could, before Mr Eckersall worked out why he had
the feeling that he had seen her before. It felt strange to
look back now and realize that in the plan that she and

Geoffrey had concocted together neither of them had given a moment's thought to the chance that someone might notice a resemblance between her and Sally. They had never been aware of it themselves. Sally's hair was not nearly as dark as Alison's and it was wavy instead of straight. Sally's face was shorter and wider and her lips were fuller. Her height was about three inches less than Alison's and she had a smaller waist, more rounded hips and far more delicately shaped feet and ankles. Yet that elusive thing, a family resemblance, must have been there in spite of all the obvious differences between them.

Alison might have made a dash for the kitchen if Mrs Eckersall had not walked into the drawing-room, saying over her shoulder, 'Alison, wouldn't you like a drink?' She added, 'Denis, aren't you going to take our bags upstairs? They're in the way there.'

He picked up two of the bags that the three of them had brought in and climbed the steep stairs. June Pullen picked up the remaining bag and followed him.

'Well?' Mrs Eckersall called out with a sound of impatience. 'Don't tell me you don't drink at all.'

Alison's hesitation had been because she had not thought out, it had just dawned on her, what her personal relationship with her employers was likely to be. Did she drink with them? Uncertainly she went into the drawing-room.

'Whisky, gin, vodka, sherry, what?' Mrs Eckersall asked.

'Sherry, please.'

'Oh God!' Mrs Eckersall said as if the mere thought of this depressed her. But she poured it out and brought it to Alison, only pausing on the way to kick off her shoes and leave them lying in the middle of the room. Her strong feet seemed to take hold of the carpet like an animal's pawing its way through soft grass. 'Let's be clear about one thing,' she went on. 'You're doing us a favour by doing our cooking for us and you eat and drink with us. No need to be shy about it. Unless you can't bear us, and if that's so, I don't blame you. Have you any objection to joining us?'

'It's very good of you to ask me,' Alison said, and felt that it was, for she wanted to hear how they talked to one another. 'But you'll remember I've a meal to cook, won't you?'

'You don't have to ask permission to go and attend to it. You come and go as you like. I may as well tell you, this is an experiment. I'd never have thought of asking that girl Linda to join us, and little Sally – I simply didn't think of it, though I tried to be motherly to her. Me, motherly!' She gave her rasping laugh. 'No wonder she left. I can't think of anything worse than being mothered by me.'

She wandered across the room to the window.

'There's Barry, still at work,' she said. 'It's incredible, the difference he's made to this garden already. How do you get along with him?'

'Quite well, I think,' Alison said, 'though it's difficult to be sure, isn't it?'

Mrs Eckersall glanced back at her over her shoulder, noticing that she was still standing.

'Sit down, sit down, don't wait to be told!' she exclaimed. Returning from the window, she sat down herself, stretching her long legs before her. 'What do you mean, it's difficult to be sure?'

'Well, are you sure yourself?' Alison took a chair facing her. 'Are you sure what he thinks of you?'

Mrs Eckersall gave her a searching look, almost as if she thought that Alison might be making a joke at her expense, then she burst out laughing.

'No, not sure at all!' She laughed again, as if Alison had said something immensely amusing. 'I must ask him.

And find myself without a gardener next day. Can't you imagine it? Do you know what my trouble is?'

From the speed at which the whisky in her glass was disappearing and remembering something that Mrs Rumbold had said on the subject, Alison could guess at one trouble, but she knew that that was not what Mrs Eckersall was talking about.

'I hate work,' she said. 'Almost all kinds of work. Think how easily I could look after the garden myself, even if my husband didn't help me much, and he wouldn't, of course. That's partly why he puts on weight so easily. And think how easily I could do the cooking here. I did at first when we bought the place. I thought it would be fun playing at being domestic. But I soon got bored. Yet with Mrs Rumbold to do the cleaning and have the place ready for us when we arrive, I oughtn't to need anyone like you at all. All the same, if you leave us suddenly, I shall become utterly hysterical for a time. I'll feel it's the end of the world, having to lift a finger to look after things. Yet I was a hard-working girl once. I was my husband's secretary and I was very efficient and I enjoyed it. But somehow idleness got into my bones. Isn't that absurd? Because I don't enjoy it. It bores me. Almost the only thing I truly enjoy is hearing myself talk. And I don't get much chance to do that when my husband's around, as you'll soon find out.'

His voice spoke from the doorway. 'Talking about the old boy? How I wish you could make up your mind what you think about him, my darling. Mrs Goodrich, don't let my wife tease you. She loves to embarrass people. It's a pastime she's developed to while away the long empty hours which my income doesn't oblige her to fill. Has she told you yet how it destroyed her, marrying a man with money?'

'I was just getting round to that when you came in and

spoilt it,' Mrs Eckersall said. 'I was just going to tell Alison what a terrible thing money is.'

'Which you don't believe for a moment, and Mrs Goodrich is too sensible to believe it either.'

They both began to laugh.

For a moment Alison took it as companionable laughter at a shared joke and she almost joined in. But each voice had a mocking edge to it which suddenly made her uncomfortable. Finishing her sherry, she said that it was time for her to see to the cooking, and made for the kitchen.

As she was crossing the hall June Pullen came downstairs. She had changed out of her jeans into a long dress of flowered cotton and put on some long gold Victorian earrings. She looked amazingly pretty.

She followed Alison into the kitchen.

'Are they quarrelling?' June asked.

'I'm not sure,' Alison answered. 'Not in the way I quarrel when I quarrel.'

'I know what you mean,' June said. 'They've their own way of being horrid to each other. I get tired of it sometimes. Were they quarrelling about me?'

'Your name wasn't mentioned.'

The girl laughed. 'But probably that's what it was really about. It's all her fault, of course. She's fantastically jealous.'

'With or without cause?'

'Does that matter? Personally I think it's stupid to be jealous, even if there is what you call "cause". Jealousy just burns you up inside. But perhaps you've never experienced it.' She watched Alison take the smoked salmon that she had bought that morning out of its wrappings and begin to arrange the slices on plates. 'Can I help?'

'Thanks, but I've hardly anything left to do,' Alison

said. She had already switched on the grill for the steaks.

June sat down on a plastic chair at the table and put her elbows on it.

'I used to be terribly jealous of her,' she said. 'She seemed to have everything anyone could possibly want, clothes and jewels and that gorgeous flat in London and this lovely house in the country and old Denis in love with her too. Or so I thought until one day he took me out and told me how she'd never loved him and didn't understand him. Of course, that was just funny, but he's got an old-fashioned way of putting things. Anyway, I realized there was no reason for me to feel jealous, I could have the lot any time I wanted it. But then I began to wonder, did I want it? I couldn't make up my mind. I'm a bit young, I think, to take such a big step, and I'd be sorry to break up their marriage for nothing.'

'I'm sure caution is wise,' Alison said.

'Now you're laughing at me. You don't believe me, do you? But it's all quite true.'

Alison started to cut slices of lemon to go with the smoked salmon.

'Do you often come down here with them?' she asked.

'Not every weekend. Just sometimes.'

'How long have you worked for Mr Eckersall?'

'About a year.'

'Then you'll have known the girls they had here before me.'

'Linda and Sally. Yes, I knew them a little. Why?'

'Oh, I just wondered what they were like. What did you think of them?'

June wrinkled her forehead. 'They were all right, I suppose. Linda had a sarcastic way of talking I didn't like. She used to tell me Louise would be grateful if I'd take old Denis off her hands, that that was why she let him bring me down here and that she'd get a good

settlement out of him and pick up with someone more
exciting. And even if she was right, which I suppose she
may have been, it used to get under my skin. That was
why she said it all, of course. She liked to get me irritated.
By the way, I don't call him Denis in the office, but he
likes me to do it when we're away from it.'

'What about Sally?'

Alison was startled by the change in the girl's face. Its
cheerful pertness disappeared. Her big brown eyes
narrowed.

'She didn't like me,' she said. 'It wasn't my fault.'

'Didn't you like her?'

'I'd no feelings about her.'

'Then I suppose you've no opinions about why she
suddenly left.'

'Why should I?'

But there was a slight tremor in her voice and suddenly
Alison had an excited feeling of having just come closer
to something far more important than anything that she
had been expecting, even though she had no idea what it
was.

She started shredding lettuce into a salad bowl.

'It wasn't that Mr Eckersall worried her by taking too
much interest in her, was it?' she asked.

June gave a derisive laugh.

'Oh God, you're as bad as old Rumbold,' she said,
'only able to think about one thing. No, I don't think he
even noticed her existence. She wasn't his type. Or is it
that business of the police coming asking questions that's
on your mind? Mrs Rumbold told you about that, I
suppose.'

'Yes, and naturally I'm curious.'

'I shouldn't be too curious if I were you.' June snapped
it out sharply. But as if she immediately regretted having
done so, she followed it with a self-conscious little laugh.

'It's just that we've all got a little tired of the subject. Her brother put the police on to trying to find her, because she didn't go home when she left here. He came down, asking questions about her himself, then managed to get the police to look into things. They were quite polite and all that, but it was a nuisance.'

'Were you down here the weekend before she left?'

'I may have been. Yes, I was. But we didn't talk much. I told you, she didn't like me.'

'Did you notice anything unusual about her?'

'I don't think I ever noticed much about her. There wasn't much to notice.'

'I mean, did she seem depressed, or excited, or anxious, or anything?'

June shook her head. 'I told you, I didn't notice anything special. She seemed just as usual to me. But perhaps if I'd thought about her more I'd have noticed something. If she was already planning to take off with the boy-friend, I suppose she'd have been a bit excited about it, wouldn't she? I've sometimes wondered who it was she went off with. Nobody seems to know.'

'Is it so certain that there was a boy-friend?'

'Well, she said so herself, didn't she? Or didn't Mrs Rumbold tell you about that? Sally left a letter for Louise and good old reliable Rumbold managed to get a peek at it and told the police all about it, and the letter said Sally was taking off with a boy-friend.'

'Was the question ever raised of whether or not Sally really wrote that letter?'

There was a pause. Then June said thoughtfully, 'God, you *are* curious, aren't you?'

'Yes, I'm afraid it's a vice of mine,' Alison agreed.

'I'd try to control it then, if you want to keep this job.' The sharp note had come back into June's voice. 'Of course, it doesn't matter what you say to me, but don't bother Denis or Louise about it, that's my advice. They got this place for peace and quiet, not to have the police prowling round their doorstep.'

'Are the police still prowling around, then?'

'Not that I know of. But I've just had an idea, a very funny idea . . .' She giggled. But the brown eyes which were intently on Alison's face had no mirth in them.

'Well?' Alison said.

'You aren't a policewoman, are you? You aren't here to investigate the case?'

Alison smiled. 'No, I'm sorry, I'm not a policewoman.'

'You're sure you aren't? It'd be such fun. You aren't here to try to find out if old Denis made away with Sally because she rejected his advances and chopped her body up and put it in a trunk and dumped it in the left-luggage office in Helsington?'

Alison had to turn away quickly because a wave of nausea suddenly washed through her and her hands began to shake. June had come so near to some of Alison's and Geoffrey's fears that she nearly lost control of herself.

June gave a peal of laughter. 'No, you aren't a policewoman. If you were one a little joke like that wouldn't have made you come over all squeamish. Do you know, you went white as a sheet?'

'I don't much like your idea of a joke,' Alison said.

'Then for God's sake, let's talk about something else. I've told you, we're all tired of that boring girl. Actually I think I'll leave you now and go and have a drink with the others.' June stood up, smoothing down her long cotton dress over her hips and giving a slight fluffing up to her curls. 'And don't go on and on about her when you talk to Denis and Louise, or I can tell you, you won't be their favourite person. Not that it matters to me.'

She left the kitchen.

Alison was glad of it. If the girl had stayed, she thought,

she would probably have betrayed herself completely by going on asking the questions that she could not have held back. For she had become certain that June Pullen knew something about Sally's disappearance. Her resentment at Alison's curiosity had been too swift and too intense to seem merely the reaction of someone who found such inquisitiveness repellent. There had been anger, and under the anger, fear. At last Alison began to feel that her coming to this house might serve some purpose.

But what was she to do next?

Her mind was a blank and she had no time to think about the problem now. She had the steaks to grill and the meal to serve. Among other things she had to lay a place for herself at the dining-table, which she did, hoping that she would hear something said that would amplify what she had picked up from June.

But nothing was said about Sally and that meal was not one to remember for its own sake with any pleasure. Even before they had sat down Mr Eckersall started talking and he talked on without stopping until the meal ended. He talked nearly all the time to Alison. She was his victim for the evening because she was a new audience and could not claim to have heard all his stories before. And unluckily for her, one of the human types that she found hardest to tolerate was the compulsive talker. Speech had been given to man, she believed, so that he should be able to exchange his thoughts with others and not so that he could bulldoze them by the appalling flow of his fluency into a desperate silence.

But she was afraid to look bored, as his wife did without any disguise. Alison did not want to antagonize him and felt that she must somehow keep up a bright, listening air, even if this brought a fleeting glint of irony to Mrs Eckersall's face, though for the most of the time she simply looked abstracted and indifferent.

Mr Eckersall talked mainly about his early life. He talked about his boyhood in a mining village in Yorkshire where his father, he said, had been a miner, bringing in good money until he had been smitten by pneumoconiosis. When that had happened he had had to be satisfied with a light job at half the wages, working the lift that took the miners down the shaft. His wife had gone out to work then as a daily in the house of one of the local doctors, but she had developed an unfortunate habit of spending most of what she earned at bingo.

'I don't want to give you a wrong idea of her,' Mr Eckersall said. 'She wasn't a gambler. She was a wonderful woman. But she was one of the people who need companionship and a bit of life. At home it was pretty grey, with my poor father coughing his lungs away and the rest of us too young to understand what the two of them were going through. She needed a little brightness and fun. I've never blamed her. Then my elder brother went down the pit and started bringing his wages home, which helped, of course. He was a splendid fellow. He was killed in a pit disaster about two years later. To be honest with you, I don't think I've ever quite got over it. I've had a kind of guilty feeling all my life that it ought to have been me, because, you see, when they started talking about me going down the pit as soon as I'd finished school, I quietly put my few belongings together and ran away. I've suffered all my life from claustrophobia. To have gone down into those tunnels would have driven me crazy. And I'd been bright at school and had other ideas about my future. I spent the next couple of years gradually working my way towards London, doing any odd jobs I could pick up. I've been a delivery boy for a grocer and a porter in a hospital and an assistant to a window-cleaner and gone from door to door, handing out samples of soap powders. And then at last I got a job as office boy in the offices of Longthorpe Pricket International and now I'm chairman. And let me tell you something odd. From the day when I first walked in at the doors of those fine offices, I knew it was going to happen. I can't explain it, but I can remember standing there in the entrance hall, which is a very impressive place with fine marble columns and black and white marble paving, and looking around and feeling that everything I saw was mine. I'd suddenly come into my own. It was an amazing feeling. Of course, it only lasted a minute, but I've never forgotten it. And through the next years, when I was a quite unimportant, though I think I may say always a very loyal employee, I never quite lost the vision.'

His wife suddenly emerged from her abstraction. 'Next time he tells you his life-story, Alison, as I'm afraid he will,' she said, 'I hope he'll remember which version he told you last. There's one about having been a curate's son who ran away to sea because he couldn't stand the restrictions of his home, and who happened to save the life of an admiral whose brother was then chairman of Longthorpe Pricket. And there are one or two other stories. If you ever find out which is true, I'd be grateful if you'd tell me. I've never got to the bottom of the matter myself.'

Mr Eckersall laughed boisterously. 'My wife has such a sense of humour. Be very careful about believing anything she tells you, Alison. Actually she knows absolutely everything about me. I'm incapable of concealment.'

'I wonder if you know everything about her,' June Pullen said, wide-eyed and innocent. She smiled with great sweetness at Mrs Eckersall.

Her stony grey eyes returned the look with expressionless fixity.

'I'm sure you wonder, June.'

'I mean, we all have our secrets, haven't we?' June said in an almost childish tone. 'I've ever so many myself

– things I simply couldn't bear to have anyone know about me.'

'Only perhaps some of those things aren't as secret as you think,' Mrs Eckersall said. 'We're often most transparent just when we think we're being cleverest at covering up.'

'Oh, I shouldn't really mind *you* knowing everything about me,' June said. 'I shouldn't mind it with people who are really my friends. You wouldn't either, would you?'

'I don't know,' Mrs Eckersall answered. 'I'm not sure that I have any friends.'

'Now just listen to her, Alison!' Mr Eckersall cried, drumming on the table with a fist and obviously feeling that the talk had got away from him for long enough. 'Didn't I tell you not to believe anything my wife says? She has swarms of friends. She picks them up right and left without any effort. I'm the lonely one in the family. I have colleagues, yes. People who are glad to consume my food and drink while they try to perusade me to give them a leg up in their jobs. That's one of the reasons we come down here, you know – to get away from parasites like that. The real peace we've got here, the simplicity and friendliness, I really don't think I could keep going without it.'

He went on to analyse at length the difference between a friend and a colleague. He also mentioned neighbours and spoke of the Fisk sisters with affectionate amusement. Alison told the story of the treacle and he roared with happy laughter.

'A thrush's nest? Bless them, bless them!' he cried.

At last the meal was over and Alison was able to clear away. She was glad that she was not invited to join them in the drawing-room for coffee. When she took the tray in to them, however, she noticed an odd thing. The flow of talk had stopped. Wondering if she had interrupted something and if they would start talking again as soon as she left the room, she lurked outside the door for a moment after she had closed it, but the silence continued.

When she had finished the clearing away, set the dishwasher going and cleaned up the kitchen, she went upstairs to her room. Sitting down by the window, looking out into the cool May night, she tried to imagine what Sally had made of the company in which she had found herself here. She herself was so direct, so open, so trusting, that the complexities of the Eckersalls and the malice of June Pullen, the antagonism between the two women and the man's enjoyment of it, would certainly have bewildered and distressed her. Alison could easily understand her deciding that she could not bear to stay.

But her abrupt leaving of the house was only half the story. The less frightening half of it. It was the problem of what she had done next and why she had not let Geoffrey and Alison know what it was that sent a chill up Alison's spine. For it was so unlike Sally. It was not natural. And thinking of June's gruesome joke about Denis Eckersall having chopped up Sally's body and put it into the left-luggage office in Helsington, Alison became almost convinced that that, or something like it, was just what must have happened. The feeling of nausea came back and she cried a little, shudderingly sure that she would never see Sally again.

But at least she was certain that June Pullen knew something about her.

All at once Alison felt so tired that she could hardly face getting up out of her chair to go to bed. She could have dropped off to sleep where she was. But for all she knew, tomorrow might be an even more difficult day to face than today had been. Yawning deeply, she made

herself get up, drew the curtains across the shiny darkness
of the windows and went to bed.

She woke early. It was the singing of a blackbird that
had wakened her. It must have been perched on top of
her bedroom chimney, for the sound came echoing down
it so that it seemed to be in the room itself, so fresh and
joyous that lying listening to it seemed the best thing that
had happened to Alison since she had arrived. But presently
the bird flew away. She looked at her watch. It was half
past six. No need to get up yet, for no one wanted breakfast before nine.

Mrs Eckersall had said the evening before that she
liked to have coffee and toast on a tray in her bedroom.
Mr Eckersall liked tea and bacon and eggs in the dining-
room. And June would get up when she felt like it and
get whatever she happened to want for herself.

But was there any reason for Alison not to get up now,
make her coffee and have it in peace before she had to
concern herself with the needs of the rest of the household? She might even take it out of doors into the sunshine
on the terrace. The sky was a clear, soft blue and there
were other birds besides the blackbird singing in the
garden. Getting up, she went to the window and leant
on the sill.

Someone was running down the steps from Barry Jones's
flat above the garage. It was June Pullen. She was in a
light flowered dressing-gown and fluffy pink slippers.
Her curls were tumbled about her rosy face. She gave a
little skip as she ran along the terrace and looked as if
she would like to break out singing like the birds. At the
porch she paused and disappeared into it on tiptoe.

CHAPTER V

MRS RUMBOLD ARRIVED on her bicycle at nine o'clock.
Alison had just taken Mrs Eckersall's tray up to her and
was frying Mr Eckersall's bacon and eggs. She had heard
him singing in his bath and had assumed that he would be
appearing shortly. In June Pullen's room there was silence.

Mrs Rumbold took off her shoes and put on her red
velvet slippers.

'Managing all right?' she asked. 'All well so far?'

'I think so,' Alison said.

'Ah, they aren't difficult, if you don't bother your head
too much about the way they talk.' Mrs Rumbold went
to the cupboard in the passage to extract the vacuum
cleaner, her dusters and polish. 'I never bother much about
the way people talk. Crazy you'd think some of them are
if you listened. I just get on with my job and take no
notice. I don't even take much notice of my Joe if he gets
into one of his states. I say to him, "You'll feel different
tomorrow," and sure enough, he nearly always does.'

Alison wondered if the states into which Mr Rumbold
sometimes got were the result of living with a woman who
never listened to him. But she did not actually believe
that Mrs Rumbold took no notice of what went on around
her. She thought that she observed and listened to everything possible with the liveliest interest. Thinking of this,
Alison remembered that there was something that she
hoped Mrs Rumbold could tell her.

'Have you ever seen a young man round here who drives
an old white Volkswagen and has a round pink face and
curly fair hair?' she asked. 'He's middling tall and I
should say he's about twenty-five.'

'David Kaye,' Mrs Rumbold answered at once. 'Has he been round? What did he want?'

'You know him then?' Alison asked.

'Oh yes, I know David.' Then Mrs Rumbold repeated the question that Alison had hoped to avoid. 'What did he want?'

'He came to the door and asked if Sally was in,' she lied. 'But when I asked him who he was, he said, "It doesn't matter," and went away.'

'That's funny,' Mrs Rumbold said. 'He knows she isn't here.'

'Who is he?'

But they were interrupted at that point by Mr Eckersall coming downstairs. He was wearing dark blue canvas shoes with thick white soles, pale blue trousers and a pale blue shirt, open at the neck and showing how white and curiously sagging the skin of it was. His thick dark hair was wet from his bath and slicked down close to his head.

'Lovely, lovely smell of bacon!' he cried. 'Ah, Mrs Rumbold, how good it always is to see you again, you dear old monster.' He gave her solid bottom a friendly smack, an action of which she seemed to be totally unaware, so it might be true to some extent that she took no notice of her employers, but just got on with her job. 'Breakfast coming up?'

'In a minute of two,' Alison said.

He made a charade of smacking his lips and went off to the dining-room.

She found him there when she took his breakfast in to him a few minutes later. He was deep in the financial pages of his newspaper and thanked her absently without looking up. She put his bacon and eggs and tea down before him and went looking for Mrs Rumbold. By then she was dusting the drawing-room.

'This David Kaye, who is he?' Alison asked.

'Runs the photographic shop in the High Street,' Mrs Rumbold answered. 'Everyone knows David. He's lived here all his life. Very clever at his work, people say. Has his pictures in exhibitions and all. Wins prizes. A nice lad. His dad's a dentist, the best in Helsington, and wanted the boy to go in for it too, but he's got this artistic side to him, you know what I mean, and that means he's stubborn, no getting him to listen to advice, has to go his own way. His dad's got a good practice and David could have gone in with him and made a good living, but he said that was no use for him. Well, I don't suppose I'd have cared much myself for spending the rest of my life looking down people's throats. Ugly things, rotting teeth. And it's terribly hard on the feet, being a dentist. I'm told most of them die young.'

Alison wondered who had told her this. She had never thought of dentistry as a hazardous occupation. But she remembered that Mark, a botanist, which certainly sounded a safe enough thing to be, had once told her that for purposes of life-insurance he was in the same category as a steeplejack. So you never knew.

'You say he knows Sally isn't here,' Alison said. 'Was he a friend of hers, then?'

Mrs Rumbold was dusting the ornaments on the mantelpiece. For all her love of talk, her work went ahead steadily.

'Remember I told you I thought I knew who her boyfriend was?' she said. 'Well, I thought it was David. She used to go out with him regular. And he did some photos of her too. She showed them to me. Lovely. They'll be getting married one day soon, I thought, and that'll be nice, they're just made for one another. Which shows how wrong you can be. There was someone else all the time I knew nothing about. And David didn't either.

When she first went away he wouldn't believe it. Came round here creating, looking as if he was ready to cry. Said he was sure something must've happened to her. Well, you know, I've sometimes wondered about that myself. *Did* something happen to her? Could she have been run over by one of those hit and run drivers, for instance, and her body dumped in a ditch where nobody's found it? Not the kind of thing you like to think about, of course, and there's that letter she wrote. I don't see how you can get round that. So I think she must've been using poor David to cover up the other fellow. For all we know, he was a real bad type and did the poor girl in right away when she went off with him. You hear of men like that. You don't expect to meet them, but you're always reading about them in the papers. And why shouldn't her family know anything about her if it wasn't something like that? Oh, I've thought about it all a lot and told most of my ideas to the police, but they didn't listen much. Girls vanishing all the time, they said, generally just to get away from their families. The families are the last people to guess there's anything wrong. But fancy David coming here again all of a sudden. Still eating his heart out, I suppose. I thought he'd given up.'

She switched on the vacuum cleaner and Alison gave up the thought of trying to talk any more against the sound of it.

Going back to the kitchen, she did the few jobs that she had to do, then took the car keys and went out to the garage.

As usual, it was open and there was another car in it now beside the old Vauxhall, a brand new, pale blue Lagonda. Barry Jones was polishing it with concentration. He did not look up as Alison opened the door of the Vauxhall, but she knew, since having seen that radiant figure running hop, skip and jump along the terrace in the early morning, that he was not as determined to be left to himself as he had made out.

Getting into the car she said, 'Good morning,' and remarked that it was a beautiful day.

Without raising his head he answered, 'I don't trust it. Feels like thunder to me.'

'Oh, surely not,' she said. 'There's such a nice fresh breeze.'

'Wait and see. I can smell thunder.' He went on with his polishing.

'How does that car compare with grass?' she asked.

'Grass?' He sounded mystified.

'You love grass,' she reminded him. 'Do you love that car? You look as if you do.'

He gave one of his mirthless smiles. 'It's part of the job. And it's a nice bit of machinery. I like most things that are good of their kind.'

Was June Pullen good of her kind, Alison wondered, as she backed the Vauxhall out of the garage. And what did she see in Barry Jones? Was he good of his kind? He was good-looking after a fashion and there was something strongly masculine about his lean, unobtrusively muscular body. And his extreme reserve might be titillating to someone who had to listen day in, day out, to the chattering of a Mr Eckersall.

When she had backed the car about twenty yards down the drive, Alison saw Miss Wendy Fisk on the Eckersalls' side of the wire fence, busily painting the grass around the briar that grew at the foot of Barry Jones's steps. Alison assumed it was with treacle. She wondered if Miss Wendy was going to leave him room to get up to his flat without getting the sticky stuff on his shoes. She was in her pixie hood and tweed coat and thick stockings in spite of the brightness of the May morning. She waved to Alison, looking very happy, like a child playing on a beach. Her sister was on the far side of the fence, painting the grass there. On a low branch of a tree near them a large ginger cat watched them with an expression of brooding malevolence.

Suddenly Alison was startled to see Miss Kitty Fisk, straighten up from her painting with a stone in her hand, which she hurled at the animal with extreme viciousness. Her aim was so good that she almost hit it. Except that its tail twitched a little, it took no notice and she resumed her painting. Alison backed out into the road and drove off to Helsington.

She had some shopping to do for the weekend and she decided to get it done before she did what she had really come to do. Parking the car where she had the day before, she went to the butcher, the greengrocer and Green and Buckley's, returned to the car, put her purchases into it, then walked slowly along the High Street, looking for a photographer's shop.

The street was crowded with Saturday morning shoppers, idling along, sometimes in groups of three or four, strung out across the pavements, so that it was impossible to hurry past them. All the same, moving as slowly as she had to, she nearly missed what she was looking for. David Kaye's shop was on an upper floor, with only one showcase at street level. Besides some conventional wedding groups and photographs of naked babies it contained one remarkably fine photograph of the old Town Hall, farther up the High Street. A staircase with an arrow on one of its walls, pointing to 'Kaye's Studio', went up between the shops on either side of it, a shoeshop and a cheap jeweller. Alison climbed the stairs, found a door with a panel of frosted glass in it on which the words, 'Kaye's Studio' were repeated, opened it and went in.

There was no one in the room inside. There was a counter across it, on which a number of framed photographs were displayed. There were others on the walls. Several of them were of Sally and although Alison could not tell how discerningly David Kaye had managed to capture the characters of his other sitters, she could say that Sally, in half a dozen of a her different moods, some of which used only to flash across her face for an instant, was so vividly, truthfully there that Alison wanted to cry out in protest at the sudden pain she felt.

Holding on to the edge of the counter, she took a deep breath to steady herself at the same moment as a grey velvet curtain over a doorway was pulled aside and the young man who had accosted her in Helsington the day before, summoned by the bell that had jangled when she opened the door, came into the room.

What immediately struck Alison about him now was how wrong her first impression of him had been. From yesterday she remembered a stocky, sturdy young man with a round, pleasant face, a very ordinary, quite unremarkable young man. And that, she thought now, was what he had been meant to be, but something had happened to him, something had gone wrong, and the truth about him now was far different. There was a fearful tiredness about the blue eyes, as if he had forgotten what a good night's sleep was. There were taut lines of strain around the wide mouth. The cheeks, which she had thought smooth and full, were drawn tight against the bone behind them. He was smiling a conscientious smile, which had been meant for a possible customer, but as soon as he saw Alison it was blotted out. Apprehension flared in the tired eyes.

'Who are you?' he demanded.

'Her sister,' Alison answered.

'What are you doing here?'

'I'm looking for her.'

'Oh God . . .' He groped blindly for one of the chairs beside the counter, sat down on it and covered his face with his hands. When he looked up his eyes were wet, but his voice, when he spoke, was low and steady. 'What can you do that I haven't done?'

'Tell me what you've done,' she said, 'and how well you knew her, and – and everything you can think of. Then I'll tell you my side of it all and we'll see if there's any way we can help each other.'

He took his time, thinking it over, then remarked in a puzzled tone, 'Your voice – it's exactly the same as hers. Do you know that? Listening to you, I can think I'm listening to her. It's almost more than I can bear. I've kept hearing her at all sorts of absurd times, you know, when she couldn't possibly have been there. And I've kept seeing her wherever I've gone. Anyone who was even faintly like her, I'd say to myself, there she is, and I'd rush up and upset some total stranger. Just as I did with you yesterday. Only there was something about you that was different from the others, and I got into my car and followed you to that house. But that gardener of the Eckersalls' was working in the garden and I couldn't make up my mind to go in. Still, the coincidence of it being the same house had to mean something, I thought, so I went back, but the man was still there and I began to think I was making a fool of myself again, because coincidences do happen all the time, and besides, I was afraid . . .'

He sank his face into his hands again.

'Afraid?' Alison said. 'Of the man?'

'Oh no, just that your being there didn't mean anything. I wanted to believe that it did. That it must. But the more I thought about it, the less likely it seemed.'

She looked behind her at the door with a glass panel in it.

'We aren't very private here,' she said. 'Anyone could walk in, just as I did. Is there anywhere else we can go?'

'There's the studio.'

'Let's go there then.'

He got to his feet and led the way to the doorway covered with the velvet curtain, holding it aside. In the room beyond there were two or three cameras on tripods, several tall white screens, a number of lamps, some high up and some on the floor, tilted upwards, and two or three chairs. If Alison had gone there to have her photograph taken she would have found it entirely normal. But because of the mood that she was in, she felt that she was entering a world of eerie abstraction, all flat white surfaces, strange, deep shadows, sharp angles and an unnatural cold white light that fell from a strip-light in the ceiling.

David Kaye seemed to become strange and not quite human, outlined blackly against the whiteness of the screens. The blue of his eyes shone out of his pallid face as if lights had been lit behind them. He pulled a chair forward for her but did not sit down himself. Standing before her, he stared down at her with as much concentration as if he were going to take her photograph, intending that it should reveal some truth about her that no one but he had perceived.

After a short silence, he said, 'You know, I can't see it now – that resemblance. It must be something in the way you move and hold yourself, because just for that instant I was certain . . . What do you want to know?'

'How you met,' Alison said. 'How well you knew her. When you last saw her. What you've done about it since. Anything you can think of.'

He began to walk up and down the room with short, jerky steps.

'We met in the public library. She dropped a book. I picked it up. She thanked me and she smiled. And I said something, I forget what, and we went our different ways.

That's all. But I couldn't stop wondering if she could smile as beautifully as that into a camera, because not many people can, you know. There's something about a camera that kills the spontaneity in their faces. They work so hard at trying to make the best of themselves that they either overdo the flashing grin, or turn stolid and dead, hating themselves because they know how badly they're doing. Three-quarters of a photographer's job is simply getting them to forget themselves. But because I went on thinking about how much I'd like the girl in the library to pose for me, I recognized her immediately when I saw her again next day, having lunch by herself in the Maytree. That's a café just across the road, where I usually have lunch myself. And I simply went in and sat down at her table and started talking. After that we took to meeting day after day when the Eckersalls weren't there. She let me photograph her as often as I liked, and cooperated beautifully, just as I thought she would. She was a perfect model. I was going to send two or three of my best portraits of her to an exhibition, but when she disappeared I hadn't the heart. I gave them to the police instead.'

He gave a short laugh and stood still, thrusting his hands into his pockets.

'They said they'd be very useful. And then they almost tore this place apart, in case she was under the floorboards. And they searched my caravan too. I live in a caravan a little way out of town. They were looking for bloodstains. I felt as if I were going mad, because it was I who'd gone to them to say she was missing. They hinted to me that that often happens, that the murderer himself puts them on his own trail. That was before your brother came down and talked to them. I'd have liked to see him if I'd known he was coming, but I only heard about him from Mrs Rumbold after he'd left. The police had me in again for

hours and hours of questioning. It was a weird sort of
nightmare to have got involved in, but to begin with I
didn't really mind, because I thought they were just doing
their job and that I ought to be glad they were being so
thorough. But once they'd convinced themselves that I
really didn't know what had happened to her, they didn't
seem to look any farther. Of course, I may be wrong
about that. They may be hunting still. But I haven't
heard anything about it.'

'When did you see her last?' Alison asked.

'We met on Tuesday the twenty-ninth of April at six-
thirty in the Seven Bells. That's a pub in Helsington
where you can get a quite good steak and chips. And
when we'd had supper we went to a cinema to see a film
called *Roads to Rome*, and after it we had coffee in the
Maytree and arranged to meet for lunch on Friday. She'd
come in by car, so she drove off home by herself. And I
never saw her again.'

'You remember it all very exactly,' Alison said.

'Of course I do. I could have given you that answer in
my sleep. The police took me through it over and over
again. I can tell you the story of the film, if you like, in
the greatest detail. I had to tell it to them several times to
convince them I'd seen it.'

'They told my brother that the last time she'd been
seen, so far as they'd been able to trace her, was on
Thursday the first of May. Mrs Rumbold saw her then in
the morning. But by the time she came again next day
Sally had gone and she'd taken all her luggage away with
her and left a letter for Mrs Eckersall. They got in touch
with us, you know, after you'd been to see them. That's
why my brother came down. But they didn't tell us who
you were, only that there'd been a query raised as to her
whereabouts.'

'Ah yes, that letter about the boy-friend she'd gone

away with.' David Kaye resumed his restless moving about the room. 'Do you believe in that boy-friend?'

'You don't?'

'I asked, do you? I've answered enough of your questions. You answer that one.'

'Then – no, I don't think I do.'

'What do you think happened, then?'

'I'm as much in the dark as you are. We've had only one idea, my brother and I, and most of the time it seems to me quite fantastic. But just sometimes it seems the only possible explanation. It's that Sally discovered something about the Eckersalls, something very dangerous to them, and that frightened them so badly that they – they got rid of her.'

'Murdered her.'

'I find it awfully difficult to say that word.'

'You may have to face it sooner or later.'

'I know.'

'And just what are you hoping to achieve here yourself?'

'I came because, if she found out this thing, perhaps I can find it out too and use it to make them tell us what happened to her.'

'If they don't decide to get rid of you too. Have you thought of that?'

'I'm afraid I think about it nearly all the time. I'm not at all brave.'

He pulled a chair towards her and sat down astride it.

'I can tell you some things about the Eckersalls,' he said.

'I was hoping you could.'

'Some are things Sally told me about them. Some are things I found out for myself after she vanished. They're fakes.'

'I think I'd realized that,' Alison said, 'though I'm not

sure just what's fake about them.'

'To begin with, those grand offices he commands – have you been told about them?'

'Yes, the entrance hall has marble columns and a black and white marble floor.'

'Only it doesn't exist.'

'All that marble?'

'All those offices. Longthorpe Pricket International Appointments have a hole-in-the-wall office in Kensington, with two or three clerks in it, a secretary and Mr Eckersall. That's all.'

'But their money isn't fake,' Alison said. 'There's plenty of it.'

'Then I don't think it comes from Longthorpe Pricket.'

'The police must know that. If they've investigated Sally's disappearance at all, they must have found that out.'

'They didn't have to find it out. I told them.'

'And they took no notice?'

He pushed his fingers through his fair, curly hair, giving her a bewildered frown. 'I don't know what they've been taking notice of. They haven't confided in me. For all I know, they still think I murdered her, but have been too clever for them.'

For all that Alison knew too, that could have been just what had happened. In deciding that it had not she realized that she was letting herself be guided by the feeling that this young man had no defences that might have concealed some dreadful violence in him. He seemed to be as open and direct as Sally herself.

'Tell me how you found out that Sally had disappeared,' she said.

'Well, as I told you, we'd arranged to have lunch together on the Friday,' he answered. 'She was coming in, just as you've done, to do the shopping for the weekend. The Eckersalls were expected in the afternoon. I went along to the Maytree and waited for her. She didn't come. I was rather worried, because it wasn't like her not to have let me know that she couldn't make it, but I supposed some complication had arisen at the house and she'd ring me up later and explain. By about six o'clock I'd worked myself into a real state because I hadn't heard anything and I tried to ring her up myself. And I was answered by Mrs Eckersall in a flaming temper. She nearly shrieked at me on the telephone. She told me Sally had left on Thursday, leaving a letter behind to say she'd gone off with some man and that there wasn't any food in the house and that they were expecting guests that evening, as Sally knew, and would I tell her please how she was supposed to manage. She'd started abusing me before she'd finished, accusing me of being the man, or at least of knowing all about it. Then she calmed down suddenly and said she was sorry, I must be as worried as she was, and rang off. And I felt as if I'd been pole-axed and after a bit I went out to the caravan, for some reason convincing myself I'd find Sally there. But of course she wasn't and I've never seen or heard anything of her since.'

'It didn't occur to you to get in touch with my brother or me,' Alison said.

'No, because of what she'd written about the man, you see. I believed it at first and thought that if she wanted you to know about it, she'd have written to you herself, and if she didn't want you to know, I wasn't going to be the one to tell you. When your brother came down, of course, I realized you were as worried as I was, but I didn't see I'd anything useful to tell you.'

'You told me one very useful thing just now,' Alison said.

He raised his eyebrows in a question.

She went on, 'You told me that according to Mrs Rumbold, Sally wasn't there when she arrived on Friday morning, yet Mrs Eckersall seems to have been taken quite by surprise when she found Sally wasn't there on Friday afternoon. She told you she'd invited guests and finding that Sally wasn't there to cope with them for her seems to have been a bad enough shock to send her into a violent temper. But don't you think Mrs Rumbold would have telephoned Mrs Eckersall on Friday morning if Sally had disappeared? After all, Sally left that letter for Mrs Eckersall, I don't know where, but it must have been propped up somewhere fairly conspicuous and Mrs Rumbold must have seen it and wondered about it, even if she couldn't read it until after it had been opened. A lack of curiosity isn't one of her qualities. She isn't a person who'd have failed to notice that all Sally's belongings were gone. I think she'd have made a fairly good guess at what was in the letter, so she can hardly have thought that Sally had just gone out shopping earlier than usual.'

'So Mrs Eckersall was playacting, was she, when she made out she was surprised at Sally being gone?'

'It could be. Only I don't know where that gets us, except that it slightly strengthens my feeling that Sally found out something about the Eckersalls which made them decide they'd got to get rid of her.'

'Found it out on Wednesday or Thursday?'

Alison nodded. 'But usually they aren't there in the middle of the week.'

'Perhaps they were for once.'

He had folded his arms on the back of the chair he was straddling. Sinking his head on to them, he seemed to retreat into his thoughts.

After waiting a moment, she asked, 'What do you know about Barry Jones?'

He raised his head. 'It's funny, I was just thinking about him. Trying to remember when he first appeared on the scene. I don't think I ever checked up. He wasn't there when Sally was working for the Eckersalls. She used to talk about what a pity it was that such an attractive garden had been allowed to get so wild. I believe she used to work in it a little herself when she had nothing else to do. But when I went to the Eckersalls' to talk to Mrs Rumbold, Jones was there, working in the garden. That was a few days after Sally vanished. I spoke to him and asked him if he'd ever seen her and he said he hadn't and that a new girl was arriving that day.'

'When I asked him if he'd ever seen you before, after you came to the gate yesterday, he said he hadn't.'

'He may have forgotten.'

'The new girl was Linda Prentice.'

'Yes, and that reminds me of something I wanted to ask you. How did you get the Prentice girl to leave? How did you get this job at all?'

'I bribed her,' Alison answered. 'I paid her to leave as suddenly as Sally had. Then I rang up Mrs Eckersall in London and told her I'd met Linda in a friend's house and she'd told me the job was going. I got it easily enough. But yesterday Linda came down and quietly blackmailed another fifty pounds out of me with the threat that she'd tell the Eckersalls how I'd actually managed things. And if I stay around for long, I expect she'll be down again.'

He suddenly reached out a hand and took a firm hold of her shoulder.

'Don't stay,' he said.

'Now I'm here, I must,' she answered.

He looked intently into her face with his bright blue, tired eyes.

'Don't. Get out. Go away.'

'But I can't.'

'Of course you can. There's no point in two of you getting – ' he hesitated, then ended the sentence in a flat tone – 'getting into trouble.'

She stood up. His hand slid from her shoulder and he used it to rake his hair back once more.

'I know you won't listen,' he said. 'But d'you realize that one of the Eckersalls has only to spot the likeness between you and Sally that I caught a glimpse of yesterday, or remember Sally's voice and think how like yours it is, for them to know that you aren't quite what you seem? They must be a bit puzzled about you anyway. You aren't a typical housekeeper, any more than Sally was. D'you know, I never understood why she took that sort of job.'

'She'd got a Diploma in Domestic Science,' Alison said, 'and she wanted to get a job as a domestic bursar in a students' hostel, or something like that, but she was rather young for it and she thought she'd fill in some time, getting experience. Earning quite good money too. She'd an idea of doing some travelling on her earnings. I don't suppose she'd have stayed long at the Eckersalls', even in the normal course of events.'

'And what about you? Don't they wonder why you wanted the job?'

'Oh, I told them a story they swallowed.'

He stood up beside her and they walked towards the doorway into the outer office.

'Well, have I helped at all?' he asked.

'I think you have,' she said. 'Have I helped you?'

'Yes – oh yes. Just to have talked – you don't know what that means.' He held the velvet curtain aside for her to pass through. 'All by myself, I've sometimes wondered if I was going mad and thought that I'd got to accept it that there'd simply been another man all the time and that if so it would be far better than all the other things that I've been thinking. Alison – your name's Alison, isn't it? She talked about you and your brother, of course. Don't take risks. And if you need me any time, send for me.'

She patted his arm. 'Don't worry about me. After all, I'm forewarned. Whatever Sally walked into, she was quite unprepared, but I've got a watchful eye on everyone.'

Words that sounded far braver than she felt. She was really in a much more nervous state after her talk with David Kaye than before it. He came down the stairs to the street with her, then said goodbye.

She looked at her watch. She ought really to have started back to the Eckersalls' by now, but she thought that she had just time to telephone Geoffrey first. Going back to the post office from which she had telephoned the day before, she dialled his home number, for as it was a Saturday he would be at home and not at the office. Probably he was only half-way through his breakfast.

When he answered she told him as briefly as she could all that had happened since the arrival of the Eckersalls, giving him the gist of her talk with David Kaye, and telling him of her feeling, which she had not mentioned to David Kaye, that Mr Eckersall was likely at any moment to become conscious of her resemblance to Sally.

She went on, 'As far as I can make out, the man's a pathological liar and he may be a crook too. It seems quite likely. He told me his whole life-story yesterday evening and his wife as good as told me that it was all invention. And David Kaye went up to London to investigate the grand offices where Mr Eckersall says he works, and found what he called a hole in the wall. I suppose that just could be a fairly harmless sort of fantasy, but he's making plenty of money somehow and I can't help feeling it's probably in some very crooked way.'

'What about this man Kaye?' Geoffrey asked. 'What do you make of him?'

'I think he's a very appealing and absolutely honest boy, desperately in love with Sally.'

'You don't think you're being led astray by charm?'

'It's possible. I'll bear it in mind.'

'And what about the gardener?'

'Well, there's one thing that worries me about him,' she said, 'apart from the fact that he's having an affair with the boss's secretary, who I'd been given to understand belonged to the boss. It's that I'm sure he's sane. I don't believe he's ever had a mental breakdown. Isn't it odd to keep ramming it down everyone's throat that you're slightly mad if you've always been as normal as anyone? I don't know much about that sort of thing, of course. He may turn into a raving lunatic at the full moon. But it would very much surprise me.'

'I don't like the sound of that,' Geoffrey said. 'I like it less than anything you've told me. What about coming home, Alison? You know, you can't really do any good down there.'

'It was your idea that I should come.'

'I have some rotten ideas. We both know that.'

'I'll think about it,' she said. 'But just at the moment I feel – yes, I feel as if I were almost on the edge of something. Now I must go, or the Eckersalls won't have any lunch. I'll telephone again as soon as I can.'

She rang off and returned to the car park.

It was true that she felt as if she were on the edge of something, though she did not know of what. Driving out of Helsington along the road that was becoming familiar, she tried to think about it, but all that she could arrive at was the fact that the relationships of the people among whom she was staying were beginning to define themselves. In another few days, she thought, she might learn a great deal more about them and that surely must illuminate something for her. Meanwhile to watch, to listen and to be unceasingly suspicious was the best that she could do.

She learnt something more about the situation in the household as soon as she turned the car in at the drive.

There were some chairs and a table with drinks on it on the terrace in front of the house. In one of the chairs June Pullen lay full length, with her arms folded behind her head. Beside her, also stretched out in a long chair, was Mr Eckersall. As Alison drove up the drive he rolled over on his side, flung an arm across June Pullen's shoulders and brought his mouth down on hers. She lay inert for a moment, then clasped his head in her hands and drew it down fiercely to her breasts, arching her body towards his.

So she had them both, Alison thought, Denis Eckersall and Barry Jones, whichever she wanted. If either.

At a window overlooking the terrace a still figure was standing. Alison was too far away to see the expression on Louise Eckersall's face, but even from where she was she could see her breathless rigidity.

CHAPTER VI

FOR LUNCH Alison gave them a cheese soufflé and a fresh fruit salad. They seemed pleased with it, but it was a far more silent meal than dinner had been the evening before. The silence emanated from Mrs Eckersall. There was something in the expressionless glances that she gave her husband and June Pullen that checked them in all attempts that they made to talk. A thunderous atmosphere developed. Yet no storm burst, at least while Alison was there.

When the meal was over Mrs Eckersall got up quickly and went upstairs. Mr Eckersall muttered something about work, told June that he would not need her and went to his study, the small room that had in it the locked walnut bureau that had interested Alison in her search of the house. June sat on for a little while at the dining-table, gazing absently before her, even after Alison had cleared it, then got up and strolled out into the garden, where she flopped down in one of the chairs on the terrace and went to sleep. Alison stacked the dishes in the dishwasher and went upstairs to her room.

There was a thunderous atmosphere there too. She thought that Barry Jones had been right in the morning when he had said that a storm was coming. The breeze had died. She could see from her window that the leaves on the trees were motionless and that the blue of the sky had developed a faintly purplish tinge. The room felt hot and airless although the window was wide open.

Sitting down beside it, she thought over her talk with David Kaye. She had trusted him without any doubts to speak of while they had been together, but now she began to wonder how guileless she had been to do so. It was her job for the present to try to cure herself of trusting anybody. And if the grim fear felt by her and Geoffrey that Sally was dead had any substance to it, wasn't it more likely to have been a sex-killing than anything else? And if it was difficult to imagine David in the role of sex-killer, wasn't that almost always said about that kind of murderer?

The other theory that Sally had stumbled on some information in the Eckersall household that made her a danger to them began to seem absurdly far-fetched. Certainly, if she had, it could have had nothing to do with their sexual relationships, for these were blatantly unconcealed. Only too apparently, they had no secrets from one another. There was nothing to betray. Alison could imagine that one day they might start killing one another, but why Sally? No, if she had discovered some sinister secret about them, it had to be something criminal.

But how could she have done that? And what was Alison to do about it?

It might have helped, she thought, if she had ever met any criminals. But in this respect her life had been very sheltered. She was aware that there are statistics about the enormous number of people in the country who have spent some time in gaol, which imply that it is almost impossible even to get on to a bus without there being at least one person on it who has been in prison. The courteous old gentleman who to one's great surprise insists on giving up his seat to one may just have finished a sentence for breaking and entering, while the stout, comfortable-looking woman, burdened with parcels, who confides in one about the aching of her feet, may be on her way home after a successful afternoon of shop-lifting. But Alison had never had the chance to discuss their vocation with any of these people and knew none of the symptoms by which someone of more experience might have recognized them for what they were.

When it came to the Eckersalls, she certainly did not know where she was. She could easily imagine that they might go in for a little tax evasion and conceivably some other kinds of fraud. But Sally's ignorance of such things was probably even more complete than Alison's. So even if she had found some incriminating evidence against them, how could she have understood enough about it to make them feel compelled to take some terrible action against her?

Alison tried to decide if she could imagine any of them as a violent person.

Yes, the answer came at once, giving her a jolt. Barry Jones.

She had been forgetting about him as she sat there brooding. But he had not come to the house until after Sally had left it, or so Alison had been told. It might not be true. Of course, it had already occurred to her that he might be a detective who was here for the same reason as herself and that he might already know far more about the Eckersalls and David Kaye and even that unknown boy-friend of Sally's, if he had existed, than Alison ever would. But would a detective start up an affair with June Pullen? Well, why not, if it helped him to get information? Or, for that matter, if he simply felt like it? It was time, Alison told herself, for her to stop thinking like a babe in the wood.

There was a tap on her door.

Before she had time to answer, it opened and Mrs Eckersall said, 'Mind if I come in?' and came in, again giving Alison no time to answer.

She went on, 'I felt like a chat. Not about anything in particular. I'm just bored. Am I interrupting anything?'

'Nothing at all,' Alison said.

Mrs Eckersall came with her long strides towards the
window, but half-way across the room she caught sight
of Mark's photograph on the dressing-table. She studied
it thoughtfully.

'Your husband?'

'Yes.'

'Good-looking.'

'In his fashion, I always thought.'

'So you're still in love with him.' Mrs Eckersall looked
at Alison with a rather contemptuous smile.

'Some habits are hard to grow out of,' Alison said.

'Even so. I'd have thought you'd have too much pride
to drag that around with you.'

'I don't put too much value on pride.'

'Don't you? Sometimes I think it's the only thing that
keeps one going.'

Mrs Eckersall turned away from the photograph and
joined Alison by the window. Looking down at June
Pullen, asleep on the terrace, she asked coolly, 'What
d'you think of that girl there? Is she dangerous?'

'To whom?' Alison asked.

'To me, of course. Who else should I be worrying about
just now?'

'I thought you might be worrying that she might damage
your husband.'

Mrs Eckersall gave her a bleak stare. 'You think I
should worry about that?'

'Well, why not? It could affect you too, couldn't it?
Even if you don't mind about the ultimate effect on him.'

'You think I ought to worry about that? I believe
you do. I come here for a chat and I get a moral lec-
ture.'

'I'm sorry,' Alison said. 'The moral tone was unin-
tentional.'

Mrs Eckersall gave an abrupt laugh. 'I suppose you want to inflict on me what you've inflicted on yourself. You make yourself carry that photograph around instead of sticking it in the dustbin and you tell yourself it's out of loyalty or something. But why should you be loyal to him if he isn't to you?'

'Suppose I want to be.'

'No, I think it's a kind of self-torture. But if you've been loyal to a man yourself, if you've earned his loyalty and he doesn't feel like paying his debt, why hug your hurt to your heart? It'll never do you any good.'

Of course it was with herself that she was arguing, though Alison was surprised that she felt so strongly about that soft-looking, pallid, garrulous man whom she had seemed obviously inclined to despise.

'I'm not sure that I've ever understood much about loyalty,' Alison said. 'Is it different from love? Unless it is, it's one of the things you can't earn. It just happens or it doesn't.'

Mrs Eckersall propped a shoulder against the window frame, still gazing down at the sleeping girl on the terrace.

'I want my debts paid,' she said sombrely. 'If you've stood by a man when he ran into trouble, even though it would have been the easiest thing in the world to give him up and even though there was pressure on you to do just that, but you felt you couldn't simply because of the trouble – do you understand me? – d'you tell me he doesn't owe you anything?'

'Something, of course,' Alison said, 'but I'm not sure what.'

She wondered who had put the pressure on Mrs Eckersall to leave her husband when he had run into what she supposed had been financial trouble, unless it had been trouble with the law. Had it been a lover with whom she had been on the point of going away? Had she given up the one thing that had deeply mattered to her and did that account for the taint of sourness and frustration that seemed to be behind everything she said?

To Alison's surprise the other woman suddenly gave a friendly grin. 'How you hate giving a straight answer to anything. What are you hiding behind all those subtle remarks? You're hiding something, aren't you?' But luckily she did not seem to expect an answer. 'Mind you,' she went on, 'I'm not asking anyone to be sorry for me. If anyone tried pitying me it'd make me mad. That's what I meant about pride being the one thing that keeps one going. It stokes up a good old healthy anger. I've been told I've a filthy temper, but if I didn't let it rip sometimes, I'd wallow in self-pity. Are you ever bad-tempered?'

'Oh yes.'

'I can't imagine it.'

Alison laughed. 'I expect it'll show itself one day.'

'What did you do before you were married? Oh yes, you told me, you took a degree in something or other.'

'Biochemistry.'

'What's your husband's job?'

'He's a lecturer in Botany in London University.'

'Have you any brothers or sisters?'

'One brother and – one sister.'

'What do they do?' She was shooting the questions at Alison as if she had not much interest in the answers. It was just a way of keeping the conversation going somehow, since she could not endure her own company for the moment.

'My brother's in advertising. My sister . . .' At that point Alison nearly made a serious mistake. She nearly said that her sister had trained in Domestic Science. But that might have stirred in Mrs Eckersall some recognition of that family resemblance which had already worried her husband. Alison had to produce one of those direct lies that always made her feel uneasy because she felt that she told them so badly. 'She's a secretary,' she said.

'Who to?'

'Oh, one of those men who write novels under half a dozen different names. I can't remember them all. His real name's Robinson.'

It was a lucky choice. Mrs Eckersall was not interested in novelists.

'I was my husband's secretary before we married,' she said, 'and that may make you wonder why I married him, because I knew him well enough. It just happened I felt I very badly wanted security. It was something I'd never had. I knew that marrying Denis wouldn't be anything wonderful, but at least I could stop worrying about the future. And I've always made it plain to him that if ever he wants to get rid of me, he'll have to come through with a very generous settlement. It's a funny thing, when I was young I used not to mind being poor and I know I got more out of life than I do now, but once you've got used to having money it's a nightmare to think of doing without it again. I could never go back to being someone else's secretary.'

'Is it really going to come to that?' Alison asked. 'Are you going to split up?'

'Oh, I didn't say that.'

'I'm sorry, I thought it was what you meant.'

Mrs Eckersall gave one of her sudden laughs. 'It's just something I think of doing about three times a day. In one of my stupider moods I talk about it. Usually the mood wears off of itself. Denis is all right. We understand one another. We each know just about how far the other will really go. Of course he's a bore and a liar and he's unfaithful, but I've known worse. I really have. Does that surprise you? My own father, for instance. What was your father like? I bet he was a vicar in some sweet little village and you loved him dearly.'

'I loved him dearly all right,' Alison answered, 'but he was an accountant in a big firm of architects. I grew up in London.'

'That's all wrong,' Mrs Eckersall said. 'You ought to have grown up in a Georgian vicarage dripping with ivy and the church clock chiming and all the rest of it. No, that's a mistake. You're really a quite tough character, now aren't you? You wouldn't let your husband get away with the things I let Denis get away with, even if you still carry his photograph around with you.'

Steering her away from this topic, Alison asked, 'What was wrong with your own father?'

'The worst thing about him was the violence in him,' Mrs Eckersall said. 'He used to bang my mother about and the rest of us too when he could catch us, but he was drunk half the time when he happened to be at home, and it made him clumsy, besides which he was lame in one leg from an accident he'd been in. He was a long-distance lorry driver. He used to bring fish down from Wick to Billingsgate. And once he crashed the lorry into a bus when he was half asleep and broke his thigh, which was lucky for him, considering. Some of the people in the bus didn't get off so well. The best thing about him was that he was away from home a lot of the time, and he made good money and my mother saw to it that we all had good educations. Not what you'd call good educations, I expect, but I got a secretarial training of a sort at the school I went to and my first job when I was fifteen. Then I got ambitious and took elocution lessons and taught myself a lot of other things besides.'

'How many of you were there in your family?'

'Eight. But I couldn't tell you what half the others are doing now. I haven't kept in touch with them.'

On the terrace June Pullen stirred, sat up, pushed her ringlets back from her face and looked upwards, as if she were suddenly wondering where the sunshine had gone. A bank of cloud so evenly dark that it looked almost solid had covered most of the sky. The stillness of the air seemed even deeper than before.

'Would you believe it,' Mrs Eckersall went on, 'that girl's got an aunt who's Lady Somebody-or-other? That is, if what she's told us about herself is true. Have you been wondering how much I've just been telling you is true?'

Alison found her trick of guessing what had been in her mind very disconcerting.

'It did just occur to me that it's awfully like the story your husband told me about his early life,' she said, 'and you said yourself that wasn't true.'

'It isn't. At least, I don't think so. Not much of it, though I've never taken the trouble to check up. But my story's true. I make things up if it'll save me bother, but generally I think the truth's much more interesting than make-believe. I don't suppose I'm any more of a liar than you are.'

As she said it her grey eyes looked straight into Alison's. It was one of those looks that could have meant half a dozen different things, all of them frightening. It set Alison's heart racing. She felt certain for a moment that Mrs Eckersall was letting her see that she was perfectly well aware what Alison was doing in her house.

Yet the look was not ill-natured. Even the trace of mockery in it seemed quite friendly and Mrs Eckersall hardly paused before she stretched, yawned and remarked casually, 'Well, I mustn't go on wasting your time. There are probably all sorts of things you want to do, write letters or read a thriller or something. I'll see you later.'

She turned away to the door, giving Mark's photograph

one more look as she went out.

The coming storm had already given Alison a headache, but the first grumble of thunder did not come until ten in the evening. She was in the kitchen, clearing up the debris of dinner, when she heard the first rumble a long way off. She had not noticed any lightning. But the kitchen was abnormally dark for that time of the evening and outside in the twilight of the garden there was a sudden wild tossing of the treetops as if they were all at once straining to escape from the fury thickening in the air.

She stood watching them for a moment, then turned towards the door, meaning to switch on the light.

Mr Eckersall was in the doorway, smiling at her.

'You like storms, eh?' he said.

He came forward, not very steadily. She did not know how much brandy he had drunk since dinner, but she thought that it must have been a good deal.

'Gives you a kick, I can see it does,' he said. 'Just like me. This one's going to be a beauty. Pray for the safety of those at sea!'

Dazzling light suddenly flared in the dimness of the kitchen.

He began counting slowly, 'One, two, three, four, five . . .'

The thunder crashed. It was much nearer than before.

'Five miles away,' he said with an air of satisfaction, as if he had just proved some difficult proposition. 'Now tell me, Mrs Goodrich – Alison – I can't get used to your being Alison, you're so bloody dignified – do you think I'm a fool?'

It would have given her a certain pleasure to say yes, but as she could hardly do that she laughed in a friendly way, as if it did not occur to her to take his question seriously.

He laughed too. 'You probably wish I was,' he said,

'but I'll tell you something, I'm not. I can tell a hawk from a what's-its-name. That cheese soufflé now that you gave us at lunch. First rate. Enjoyed every mouthful. Only not as good as she could make it. Not quite, quite – well, I don't know the word for it, but it hadn't got something or other that hers had. Understand me?'

At first Alison did not. She was slow. She thought that he was merely drunk and did not know what he was saying. Then she realized that although he certainly was drunk, he knew what he was saying only too well.

He was watching her with a broadening grin, enjoying the look of shock that had appeared on her face.

'It was the cheese soufflé that clinched it,' he said softly, with an almost tender sound in his voice that sent a shiver up Alison's spine. 'I suppose one of you gave the recipe to the other. Clever of me to think of that, wasn't it? I was puzzled about you from the start, then I remembered the girl made a soufflé just like it for us one day. It was perfect. I went out of my way to compliment her on it. Asked her to make another soon. She blushed like a rose. You've gone dead white, d'you know that? White as a sheet.'

'Well?' Alison said with a touch of bravado.

She thought that the oblique way in which he had referred to his discovery meant that he wanted to get as much fun as he could out of the situation.

He gave a giggle, came up close to her and put an arm round her waist.

'"Well?" she says!' He rubbed his cheek against hers. 'Is that the only word you know? You come snooping into our house, we let you in in good faith, we fall over backwards trying to be nice to you, hoping you'll stay with us for ever and ever, and then when it turns out you aren't all you seem to be, all you can say is, "Well?" D'you know what I call that?'

She never found out what he called it, because the lightning flashed again. It made a great jagged gash in the blackness of the sky.

He immediately started counting. 'One, two, three . . .'

The sound of the thunder seemed to rock the room.

'Three miles off,' he said, letting go of her and going to the window. The rain came suddenly in a torrent, making a loud crackling noise as it slapped against the glass and hissed on the stones of the terrace. 'It'll soon be here. But d'you know, you don't really hear the thunder when it's right on top of you? Not as you think of thunder. It sounds like a great whip being cracked. Have you ever been at the heart of a storm?'

She had a feeling that she might be at the heart of one now, even if it was not the one that he was talking about at the moment.

'I'm not sure that I have,' she said.

Turning towards her again, he repeated his little giggle.

'Ah ha, she isn't sure. So many things she isn't sure about, like what I'm going to do about what I've just found out about her. Well, I'll tell you something, I'm not sure myself. I'll have to think. I'm not much of a thinker in the ordinary way, but now and again I go into things very deeply.'

'Will you tell me one thing?' Alison said. 'Does your wife know about this?'

'Not unless she's found it out for herself. I haven't said anything to her yet. Lots of things I don't say to her. Why? Would it worry you if she did know?'

'No, it's just that . . .' Alison sat down at the table, put her elbows on it and hid her face in her hands. She was half acting and half meant what she said. 'I feel terrible for having tried to take you in. You've all been so nice to me, and your wife especially. But do please understand how awful things have been for us – my brother and me.

We didn't know what on earth to do. Sally came here and then simply vanished. And we never believed in that letter of hers about a boy-friend. I don't mean she didn't have boy-friends. She was such a charmer, she had more than she could cope with. But she was never in the least secretive about them. To have gone off with one of them and not even write to us about it – I mean, to *us* – just didn't seem real. So I came looking for her. But of course it was a mad thing to do.' To her surprise she found some real tears welling up in her eyes. 'I'll go away tomorrow – this evening – if you like.'

'For Christ's sake, don't do that!' he said, sounding astonished. 'Louise would just about kill me if she knew I'd frightened you away. What does it matter if you *are* that poor girl's sister? But I do assure you . . .' He laid a hand on her shoulder and spoke with alcoholic solemnity. 'I assure you she did write that letter. I saw it myself. It's obvious she got herself into trouble of some kind. Could be some sex-maniac got hold of her and she's dead, buried . . .' His voice suddenly became harsher. 'But it isn't in this garden, if that's what you've been wondering about. Everything's dead normal here, I can promise you that. I've done some worrying about her myself, you know, ever since your brother came here, in case the thing was somehow my fault. Could be she took some joke of mine in the wrong spirit and felt she'd better run away, run away from me to this fiend, whoever he was. Terrible thing to have on my conscience.' His voice had grown maudlin and trembled as if he too were about to start crying.

The thought of what his wife would make of it if she were to come into the kitchen and find the two of them in tears made Alison brush her own away.

'Of course what I ought to have done,' she said, 'was come to you and tell you openly about our worries.' And a lot of good that would have done, she thought. However, putting as much sincerity into her voice as she could, she went on, 'Then I expect you would have helped me to search for her. But how could I know you'd be so wonderfully kind and understanding?'

The lightning flashed again and he began absent-mindedly to count, 'One, two, three, four . . . Going further away.' He sounded regretful, as if something in him ached to feel the climax of the storm. 'The question is now, what are we going to do about you? Do you stay on as our cook, wondering if we're murderers? Queer thing to have to ask oneself, you must admit that.'

'Oh, I do, I do,' she said, 'and I'll go away – '

'No!' he roared. 'Not till I've had time to think. That is, I must do some thinking tonight and see how I feel about things in the morning. Don't you try anything on till I tell you, d'you understand me?' There was an unmistakably threatening note in his voice now. His pasty-looking face turned a purplish red. 'Don't think of going to the police with stories about us. Don't try to bring in the Press with nasty innuendoes and smears. Just go to your room and stay there quietly till I've had time to think. Go on – go!'

She got up and went upstairs to her room.

As she closed the door her glance went to the keyhole. She had a feeling that she would like to lock herself in that night. But there was no key. She thought of propping a chair under the doorhandle, as she had seen people do in films, but decided that it would probably not provide much protection if a determined Mr Eckersall wanted to get into her room and murder her. In any case, she thought, the sudden fear of him that she had felt in the kitchen when he had started shouting at her was mainly hysterical. Sober, he seemed harmless enough.

Yet the feeling of fear did not quite subside. The

abruptness with which his mood had changed might have been the result of too much brandy, but that did not necessarily make it less dangerous. In fact, as he sobered up, he might become less good-natured than he had been drunk.

The important question remained what the truth was about what had happened to Sally. If he had a load of fear and guilt on his mind it might seem as important to him to get rid of Alison as it had, for whatever mysterious reason, of Sally. On the other hand, he must realize that it would not look too well if too many members of Sally's family kept disappearing from his house. If he discussed the matter with his wife, Alison felt sure that she would point that out.

All the same, if it had not been for the storm, she would probably have packed her suitcases and quietly left the house. Any usefulness her stay there might have had was at an end. The sooner she got away, the better. But as she listened to the battering of the rain against her window, which sounded almost as if it might break the panes in, she realized that she would be soaked to the skin before she reached the end of the drive.

The storm had come very close again. The thunder followed almost immediately on the lightning. The old house creaked and groaned. But the sound for which she could not stop herself listening was the very soft one of a stealthy footstep on the landing. Half a dozen times she thought that she heard it and sat rigidly staring at the doorhandle, waiting to see it turn. But nothing happened.

In fact, she heard no footsteps or voices at all and after a time began to feel almost as if she must be alone in the house. That was absurd, of course, for who would go out on a night like this? And at last she heard Mrs Eckersall's bedroom door open and close and not long after that of her husband's, and then June Pullen came upstairs, cheerfully singing to herself as she passed Alison's door. There was no stealthiness about any of them. At last she got undressed and went to bed herself.

The storm slowly died, but it was midnight before it ended. Even then Alison could not sleep. She knew that she must leave in the morning, but meanwhile her thoughts kept going round and round in circles as she tried uselessly to convince herself that she had discovered something of at least a little value. But she had not picked up the smallest trace of Sally. The Eckersalls seemed to think her disappearance unimportant. The police appeared to have made a few inquiries about her, then given up. Only David Kaye cared in any way. And she must leave in the morning . . . There she was, back to the start.

She slept later on, but it was only shallow sleep, made frantic by dreams. She was glad to wake and at about seven o'clock she got up, had a bath, dressed and packed her suitcases. She would go downstairs, she thought, make herself some coffee, then help herself to a sheet of paper from Mrs Eckersall's writing-table and leave her a note, telling her to ask her husband why she had left, always supposing that he had not already done so. Then Alison would write that she was borrowing the Vauxhall to get to the station and that Mrs Eckersall would find it parked there.

Or ought she to walk? Would it be putting herself too hopelessly in the wrong to help herself to the car? No, she was not going to walk three miles, carrying her cases, with not much hope of thumbing a lift. And it would be hardly any trouble for one of them to drive Barry Jones to the station in the Lagonda to pick up the other car.

Going downstairs quietly, Alison went to the kitchen and started to make the coffee.

She had only just started to drink it when the front-door bell rang.

She had a feeling, even before she went to answer it, that the only people likely to come calling at such an hour were the Fisk sisters, and there they were in the porch, Miss Kitty standing as usual just behind Miss Wendy, their shoulders touching and both of them looking as if this contact gave them support that they needed badly. Both of them were shaking and their wizened faces, under their pixie hoods, were even paler than usual.

For a moment, before Alison had taken in that they were both in a state of intense terror and shock, she thought that they must have come to tell her that the ginger tom had penetrated their defences of treacle and gobbled up the little newly hatched birds in the nest in the rose bush. Then, as Miss Wendy's little hard hand shot out and grasped Alison's sleeve, she recognized that even they would not look as they did if that was all that had happened.

'Come with us, come with us!' Miss Wendy croaked. 'Come and see. That man who was here in the car last night, he's shot poor Mr Jones. Shot and killed him. Oh, Mrs Goodrich, come with us quickly and tell us what to do.'

CHAPTER VII

ALISON WENT with them. Their fear invaded her, though she could not believe in what they had said. Close together, they pattered ahead of her along the terrace. They reached the bottom of the steps that led up to the flat above the garage. There they both stood still and looked at her with an air of challenge, like two children daring her to go further. The possibility that what they had said was true began to penetrate her own sense of shock. She stiffened, feeling unable to move, then took the stairs at a run.

The door of the flat was open. Barry Jones's body lay in a huddle just inside it. She took only one quick look, then stepped back, leaning against the stone parapets, shutting her eyes, as if that would help to shut out what she had just seen, and felt nausea rise convulsively in her throat.

Most of the dead man's face had been blasted away. One eye, half out of its socket, stared at her out of a morass of blood and bone on which a bluebottle crawled luxuriously. For some reason she clung to a doubt that he really was Barry Jones. There had been little to recognize him by except the redness of his hair, and it might have been a little easier to face the horror if he had been a stranger. But while she stood there, not daring to take a second look and with coloured sparks dancing in front of her fast-closed eyes, she knew that there was really no question of who he was. A man who was almost as much of a stranger to her as the complete stranger that she had hoped he was. A man who loved grass. That was about the only thing that she was sure she knew about him.

She had seen into the room behind him, but had not taken in anything about it except for an impression of great neatness. So there could have been no struggle in there. She had noticed too that the dressing-gown and pyjamas that he was wearing were soaking wet and that there was a puddle of water on the floor, where it must have rained in. So it had happened before the storm ended. Someone had come up the stairs and, still standing outside, had shot Barry Jones point blank when he opened the door. Not that these things interested her at the moment. Nothing interested her but her struggle with her sickness and faintness.

She managed to get down the stairs again without giving in to either. The Fisk sisters had not moved. They watched her come down to them with their eyes identically wide and questioning. She steadied herself against the bottom of the parapet.

'How did you find him?' she asked.

'It was the mirror on the stairs,' Miss Wendy answered.

'And, of course, the storm,' Miss Kitty added.

'A mirror? You mean you could *see* . . .?'

Alison looked at their house in the midst of its wilderness of a garden and wondered what they could mean. Even leaning far out of any of their windows, it would have been impossible for them to see Barry Jones, collapsed in his doorway, and a mirror inside the house would hardly have helped them.

'No, no,' Miss Wendy said, 'not until we came round this morning.'

'You came to see him this morning?'

'Yes, about the mirror. It crashed in the night. It's a miracle, really, that it isn't broken. But it came down with a great crash and as my sister was saying, we didn't take any notice at the time because of the storm. We thought the noise was just part of the thunder. It was only when we were going up to bed that we found the mirror lying at the bottom of the stairs. It's a very big mirror, you know, Florentine, with a very fine frame and quite valuable. And it's been hanging there on the stairs ever since we were little girls and I don't suppose either of us has ever given a thought to how it hung there.'

'I'm sure I never have,' Miss Kitty said. 'Not a thought. It felt like a part of the house.'

'Well, it hung on a piece of wire,' Miss Wendy went on, 'on some hooks plugged into the wall. And the wire broke. After all these years it just broke. Rusted through. And we couldn't think what to do about it once we'd picked it up and propped it against the wall. It's terribly heavy, you see. It was quite difficult for us to lift it. Then we didn't go to bed after all, because we stayed up discussing what steps we ought to take to have it hung up again. We thought of calling in a joiner, but we don't trust the local tradesmen, I'm afraid. They're all cheats and robbers. They send in great bills for work they've only pretended to do, thinking because we're just two old women they can get away with anything . . .'

At the top of the steps a man was lying murdered. At the bottom Miss Wendy went on telling Alison about the villainies of the local tradesmen until, half dazed, she interrupted.

'But why did you come here?'

'Because in the end we decided that the best thing we could possibly do would be to consult Mr Jones,' she said. 'He's always been most obliging. He changed a spare wheel for us once when he saw us struggling with it, and sometimes he's given us lifts into Helsington so that we haven't had to get the car out. As a matter of fact, he told us it wasn't really safe to drive it any more because the clutch won't operate, which had never occurred to us. And look at the way he advised us how to deal with that horrible ginger tom. So we thought we'd come over and ask him if he'd be so very kind as to hang the mirror up for us again. We were sure he could do it quite easily, he's so very clever. And we came over and we – and we found – '

Memory of what they had found seemed suddenly to return to her. She snatched a terrified glance at the stairs and her face crumpled.

As if moved by identical feelings, Miss Kitty's face crumpled too.

'We found him dead, murdered,' they both wailed.

'But it's so early,' Alison said stupidly. She knew that she ought to have made up her mind what to do, but the cloud of words was confusing her. 'I mean, didn't you think it was awfully early to be disturbing him about a little thing like your mirror?'

'We wanted to get it settled and go to bed, you see,' Miss Wendy said. 'We've been up all night, trying to decide what we ought to do. We didn't want to exploit Mr Jones. We don't think one should exploit a person simply because he's already been kind. So we tried telephoning one or two joiners we found in the yellow pages, but we only got the rudest replies, literally asking us if we were mad, ringing up at that hour. Can you imagine such rudeness? And with us so worried. I said it was an emergency, but they only said – oh, I can't bring myself to repeat it. So in the end, when we'd had some tea, we decided to come over and talk to Mr Jones and after that, when he'd told us what to do, to go and get some sleep. And that's what I think we'll do now, if you don't mind, as you know everything and I'm sure can manage without us. We're both very tired.'

They looked very tired, but Alison took a firm hold of Miss Wendy's arm, in case she and her sister should try to slip away.

'I don't think you'd better go yet,' she said. 'You'll have to tell all this to the police. And of course to Mr and Mrs Eckersall. I'll go and wake them. But didn't you tell me something about seeing a car in the drive and a man get out of it during the night?'

'We didn't actually see a man,' Miss Wendy said, 'but if there was a car there, there must have been a man in it, mustn't there?'

'Or a woman,' Miss Kitty said.

'Yes, of course, it could have been a woman,' Miss Wendy agreed. 'Or perhaps there were several people. We don't know.'

'But you did see a car?'

'Oh yes.'

'When was this?'

Miss Wendy looked fretful. Time was clearly not a matter that she was able to think about with any clarity.

'During the storm,' she said. 'We were looking out of the window at the lightning and we saw the car standing in front of the garage. We saw it in a flash of lightning.'

'So it was after dark,' Alison said. 'Fairly late.'

'Yes, I suppose it must have been.'

'Well, come along now and I'll wake the Eckersalls and I'll make you some more tea while we're waiting for the police.' She steered them back along the terrace to the porch. 'They'll want to know all about the car and the mirror and everything.'

'But we're so tired,' Miss Wendy protested.

'Yes, I can't think when I've ever felt so tired,' her sister said.

'All the same, I think you should stay,' Alison said and was thankful that they did not resist as she led them into the house and into the drawing-room.

Hoping that they would not flit away while she was waking the Eckersalls, she left them seated side by side on the sofa, then ran upstairs and went to Mr Eckersall's door. For some reason it seemed natural to wake the man of the house first, though if she had stopped to think about it, she would probably have gone to his wife. Alison thought of her as the more sensible, the more practical, the less excitable. But she did not stop to think.

Pounding on his door, she called out, 'Mr Eckersall! Wake up! You're needed downstairs immediately!'

She heard him give a grunt and mutter angrily, 'Who the hell's making that bloody noise? Go away!'

She knocked again. 'Mr Eckersall, it's about Barry Jones. He's dead.'

'He's what?' came the drowsy voice again.

'Dead,' she said. 'Dead.' She saw no point in trying to break the news gently.

'You're talking nonsense.'

'No, it's true. Please come.'

'Wait!'

There was silence inside the room. Then she heard bare feet padding towards the door. Mr Eckersall opened it. He was in a short black and yellow striped dressing-gown over yellow pyjamas and was tying the belt of the dressing-gown as he looked out at her.

'This isn't some bloody awful joke?' he said. 'You mean it? Barry's dead?'

'Yes.'

'How d'you know?'

'The Fisks found him. They went to ask him what to do about some mirror of theirs that fell down in the night, then they came and fetched me. He's there in his flat. He's dead. I think he's been shot.'

'Just a minute.' He turned back into the room, hunting for his bedroom slippers. After a moment he came out on to the landing.

'Shall I wake Mrs Eckersall?' Alison asked.

'You've probably done that already with all this row,' he said. 'She'll come down when she wants to. Come on, show me.'

He went ahead of her down the stairs.

As they went out through the front door she had a glimpse through the open door of the drawing-room of the Fisk sisters, sitting exactly as she had left them, like two children who have decided to be good. She followed Mr Eckersall out on to the terrace. But she saw no reason to inflict on herself again the sight of the dead Barry Jones and as soon as she had seen Mr Eckersall begin to mount the steps to the flat, she turned back into the house, went to the kitchen and began to make the tea that she had promised the Fisks.

Her coffee had grown cold and she poured it down the sink, took several cups out of the china cupboard and prepared to make tea for the whole household. The kettle was just coming to the boil when she heard Mr Eckersall come running into the house.

He went straight to the telephone in the study and, Alison supposed, dialled 999, for a moment later he was shouting, 'Police! Yes, I want the police. Yes, yes, it *is* an emergency. I want the police!'

He was still shouting when Mrs Eckersall came into the kitchen.

She was also in a dressing-gown, a frilly white cotton one which made her look much younger than usual. She had waited to pull a comb through her pale gold hair and she must have paused in the hall to listen to what her husband was saying on the telephone, for she seemed to know what had happened.

'It's true then, is it?' she said. 'Barry's dead?'

'Yes,' Alison answered.

'Shot? Murdered?'

'That's what it looks like.'

'That's what I thought I heard you say upstairs.' There was an unnatural equanimity about the way Mrs Eckersall spoke, but her face was very pale. 'If that's tea you're making, make some for me.'

'There's no need to make tea for us,' Miss Wendy said, suddenly appearing with her sister behind Mrs Eckersall. 'We only want to go home. Now that Mr Eckersall has taken charge and the police are coming, there's no need for us to remain. Of course we'll be available to the police any time they want us.'

'No, no, sit down!' Mrs Eckersall cried commandingly. 'Of course you must have some tea. Sit down – I'm sorry, I should have said good morning, thanked you for coming. It was so good of you. But this is such a shock, I hardly know what I'm doing.'

'I should like a cup of tea,' Miss Kitty said, for once taking the initiative and sitting down at the kitchen table. 'Seeing that it's just ready and if it's no trouble to anyone.'

'Of course it's no trouble,' Alison said and began pouring out the tea.

'So the police are coming,' Mrs Eckersall said thoughtfully as Alison handed her a cup. 'Again. They'll be getting tired of us. They came, you know, when Sally disappeared. I wonder if this awful thing today is somehow connected with that. If too many awful things happen to one it can hardly be coincidence. Poor Barry, I always rather liked him. I wonder who had it in for him.'

Her voice was still abnormally level and calm.

'Miss Fisk can tell you about a car she saw come here last night,' Alison said. 'It might be important.'

'We didn't see it *come*,' Miss Wendy corrected her as she sat down beside her sister. 'It was late when we saw it outside the garage, but we didn't see it arrive. It might have been there for hours.'

'A car?' Mrs Eckersall said. 'What kind of car?'

'Oh, I couldn't tell you a thing like that,' Miss Wendy answered. 'I can't tell one car from another. It wasn't very big.'

'But it wasn't very small either,' Miss Kitty said.

'What colour?' Mrs Eckersall asked.

They both shook their heads.

'We don't know,' Miss Wendy said. 'We saw it just in a flash of lightning and of course we weren't particularly interested at the time, because why shouldn't Mr Jones have visitors if he wanted them? Or you? Naturally we didn't know who the owner, whoever he was, had come to see, you or Mr Jones or even Mrs Goodrich. It was only this morning, when we found poor Mr Jones dead, that we began to think about the car. Of course we shall tell the police all about it.'

'Yes, I should do that.' Mrs Eckersall was spooning sugar into her tea. Normally she avoided it in both tea and coffee. She had very personal ways of showing her sense of strain. When she sipped the tea she grimaced at its sweetness, but went on drinking it.

'The car was a light-coloured sort of car,' Miss Kitty said suddenly.

'Tell me about how you found him,' Mrs Eckersall demanded.

Almost in unison the sisters began to pour out the story that they had already told Alison and in almost the same words. But before they were half-way through it Mrs Eckersall had grown impatient and in the middle of one of their sentences strolled away into the passage as if she were going looking for her husband.

Actually, as she must have heard, he had left the house again and returned to where Barry Jones lay.

From a little way along the passage Mrs Eckersall called out, 'Alison!'

Alison followed her out.

Mrs Eckersall put her mouth close to her ear and hissed in a fierce whisper, 'For God's sake, get rid of those two awful women! They make my flesh creep. A couple of hundred years ago they'd have been burnt as witches and a good thing too. I'm going upstairs to get dressed now. Mind they're gone by the time I come down.'

'What about June?' Alison asked. 'Oughtn't we to wake her?'

'If she can sleep through the row we've been making, let her sleep.' Mrs Eckersall gave a short, strange laugh.

The sound of it made Alison's flesh creep a little. If witches were still burned, she thought, there was a possibility that this woman herself might not escape. It was obvious, anyhow, that she knew of June Pullen's visits to the flat above the garage. Waiting in the passage until she began to climb the stairs, Alison returned to the kitchen.

She had less difficulty in persuading the Fisk sisters to leave than she had had in persuading them to stay. They had already drunk the tea that she had poured out for them, had stood up and were only waiting for her to come back to take a polite farewell.

'Thank you for the tea,' Miss Wendy said. 'It's done us both good. Now we'll go home. But we shan't go to bed in case the police want to talk to us, as I expect they will. It's all dreadfully sad, isn't it? As I've told you, we liked Mr Jones so much and what the Eckersalls will do without him I simply can't imagine. He made such an improvement in the garden and I can't really see Mr Eckersall keeping it up. But that reminds me, at least one nice thing has happened on this terrible morning. Just come along with us and we'll show you.'

Alison did not want to go with them. She had seen as much of them as she wanted. But each sister grasped her firmly by an arm and both looked up into her face with such suddenly happy smiles that it chilled her blood. She

began to feel that Mrs Eckersall had been right about
them and that they were witches. Who else could smile
so radiantly with the smell of blood in their nostrils?
What horror did they want her to see?

But all that they wanted to show her were the newly
hatched little thrushes in the nest in the briar patch.

'Don't worry about the treacle getting on your shoes,'
Miss Wendy said as they led Alison up to the bush.
'The rain washed it all into the ground. Such a waste
and of course we shall have to buy some more as soon as
we can. Meanwhile we'll keep watch to see that that
horrible Colonel Mayberry doesn't eat the dear little
things. Now look.'

With a horny little hand she delicately parted the leaves
and thorny stems.

With loud and angry squawking, the mother thrush
rose from the nest, revealing four great open beaks inside
it, attached to pink, helpless-looking bodies with lungs
that moved like bellows.

'Aren't they heavenly?' Miss Wendy said in an awe-
struck whisper.

'Heavenly!' her sister breathed.

'But we mustn't stay or we'll frighten the poor mother
away from them.' Miss Wendy very gently let go of the
twigs that she had been holding and stepped back. 'Now
goodbye, Mrs Goodrich. I expect we'll see you later.'

The sisters climbed through the fence and trotted away
to their own house.

Alison turned back to the porch. Mr Eckersall was
sitting on the bottom step beside the garage. He did not
speak to her. The garage doors, as usual, were open and it
happened that she saw something to which she gave no
thought at the time, though it must have made some
impression on her, puzzled her or somehow disturbed
her, since later she remembered it as clearly as she did.

It was simply a small puddle of water directly under
the dangling nozzle of the long green plastic garden hose
which was attached to a standpipe in the garage and was
hung up in coil upon coil on a hook high up on the wall.
It looked as if someone had been using the hose recently.
Yet it could hardly have been to water the garden, for the
ground outside the garage was still sodden from the storm.

The police arrived soon afterwards. Alison went out on
to the terrace to see what they did. They came in two
cars, but only a few minutes after the man who appeared
to be in charge had disappeared up the steps into Barry
Jones's flat, a sergeant came towards her and asked to
be allowed to use the telephone.

She took him to the telephone in the little study. That
was when she noticed that the flap of the walnut bureau,
which had been locked when she searched the room on
Thursday, was open now. There was absolutely nothing
inside it. She left the sergeant there. He must have summoned reinforcements, for it was not long before the cars
of a doctor, a photographer and some other men with
various kinds of equipment drove up the drive. Alison
stayed in the kitchen, making more tea and cutting some
bread and butter, because she had just realized that she
was extremely hungry. She had begun to feel that she
had been up for hours and temporarily she had quite
forgotten that she had meant to leave the house that
morning. She had forgotten her packed suitcases upstairs
and the talk that she had had with Mr Eckersall the
evening before.

Her mind was mainly on Sally. She had no evidence
that the murder of Barry Jones had any connection with
Sally's disappearance, but as Mrs Eckersall had seemed
to wonder, if one murder could happen here, why not
two?

If this was not a logical way of thinking, Alison found

it dreadfully convincing. The theory which up till then she had taken only half-seriously, that Sally had stumbled upon something criminal and had been made away with to stop her talking, seemed suddenly horribly likely to be close to the truth. Alison began to feel impatient to talk to the police to make sure that they remembered the girl who had vanished from this house.

Before she could talk to the police, however, June Pullen, in jeans and her sloppy sweater, came running down the stairs and burst into the kitchen with a frantic demand to be told what was happening. So Alison had to go over the story once more for her. After the first look of shock, June's pert little face went white with fury, or that was what Alison took the blaze in her eyes and the twitching of her mouth to mean as she rushed past Alison and out into the garden.

A minute or two later Mrs Eckersall reappeared, saw Alison eating bread and butter and said, 'You can give me some of that. Nerves always make me hungry.'

Alison cut and buttered a slice of bread for her and she started eating it with swift, savage bites. She had dressed more formally than usual in a very plain dark grey linen dress and had twisted up her pale hair into a roll at the back of her head, as if she felt that this was appropriate for an interview with the police.

Suddenly she shot one of her sharp questions at Alison. 'D'you ever go in for premonitions?'

'I don't think so – not really,' Alison said. 'Sometimes I think I've had one that's turned out right for once, but then I've remembered all the times they haven't.'

'Yes, I know, that's how it is with me. I don't really believe in them.' Mrs Eckersall frowned musingly, as if something passing through her own mind bewildered her. 'All the same . . .'

'Yes?' Alison prompted her.

'Oh, it's nothing. A feeling I've had the last few days.'

'That something like this was going to happen?'

'Not necessarily like this. Not anything like a murder. Just something awful. I've been fearfully worried about a lot of things recently. You've seen that, of course.'

'I couldn't help seeing it.'

'And now I suppose you'll tell the police about it. Not that it matters. But are you going to tell them about why you came here?'

'So you know about that,' Alison said. 'Your husband told you last night after all.'

'Yes, Denis is quite clever sometimes. He told me he'd been worrying about you ever since he saw you.'

Alison sat down at the table. 'I'm feeling rather a fool.'

'There's no need for that.' Mrs Eckersall sat down facing her. 'It was a good idea you had. It might have got you somewhere if Denis or I had known anything about your sister. And even though we didn't, it's just possible, isn't it, that Barry did? There's just one thing I'd like you to tell me.'

'Yes?'

'That husband of yours . . .'

'Yes?'

'Does he exist?'

'Oh yes.'

'But you aren't separated, are you? Your wonderfully well-balanced, unrevengeful way of thinking about him, that was just a fake.'

'I'm afraid so,' Alison said. 'He just happens to be away. He's on a botanical expedition to a rain forest in Brazil. But making you think we were separated seemed a good way of explaining why I suddenly wanted a job.'

'It doesn't matter. I was just curious. Does he know you're here?'

'No.'

'Does he know about Sally vanishing?'

'He knows she left you suddenly. That happened just before he went away. But he doesn't know how long it is since we've heard from her or how worried we've been.'

'Why haven't you told him?'

'Letters take an awfully long time to reach him. And I didn't want him worrying and thinking he ought to come home. He'd been looking forward to the expedition for so long, and since my brother and I didn't even know for certain that there was anything seriously wrong, I didn't want to bring him back.'

'Your brother – that's the Mr Burnaby who came down to see us, isn't it?'

'Yes.'

'Well, I'm glad all that's cleared up.' Mrs Eckersall leant back in her chair. 'I knew you were hiding something. I hoped I could find out what it was, because I'd taken a liking to you. I thought we could be friends – '

She broke off as footsteps sounded on the terrace.

A moment later Mr Eckersall, accompanied by a tall man, appeared in the kitchen doorway.

He introduced the tall man as Detective-Superintendent Ditteridge. He looked a quiet sort of man with close-cropped grey hair and a remote, almost inattentive way of meeting your eyes, overlaid by an air of good-natured courtesy. His restless, light brown eyes never dwelt on anything for long. While Mr Eckersall was saying that the superintendent would like to talk to everybody in turn, they were snatching swift glances here and there about the kitchen, taking in, Alison felt sure, far more than most people would have noticed in twice the time, even though there was nothing there likely to be of any special interest to him.

He would like to start his questioning, he said, with Mr Eckersall. The two of them went away to the study.

After some time Mr Eckersall emerged and told his wife to go in. He took no notice of Alison but went straight out into the garden where she saw him and June Pullen standing close together on the terrace, talking fast and earnestly to one another. There seemed to be policemen everywhere. Alison stayed in the kitchen, drinking more tea and wanting to telephone Geoffrey to tell him what had happened.

But at least until she had asked the superintendent whether he had any objection to her doing this, she thought it better to postpone it. She supposed that she would not be allowed to go home that day, so it would be just as well for her to unpack her suitcases. But there was no hurry about doing it. Waiting to be summoned to the study, she felt numb and stupid. The ease with which the Eckersalls had found out who she was had given her a shock. However, as things had turned out, did it matter? Even if she had succeeded in taking them in for a little longer, she would have had to tell the truth to the police.

When she was called to the study after Mrs Eckersall, Alison found Mr Ditteridge seated at a small table in front of the window, with a large sergeant on a chair in the corner of the room with a notebook on his knee. The flap of the bureau was still open, showing its emptiness. Mr Ditteridge asked her some routine questions about her name, address and the nature of her employment with the Eckersalls, after which, without waiting to be asked any more, she went straight on to tell him of her relationship with Sally and to say that she was sure he knew her story.

He nodded and said that it had come to his attention and that they would talk about that in a moment, but that first he would like to ask a question. What references had Alison supplied when she applied for the job here?

She was puzzled and answered, 'None.'

'Mrs Eckersall didn't ask you for any?'

'No, she said anyone could fake them and she preferred to go by people's faces.'

'And that seemed to you normal?'

'Why not? A lot of people feel like that.'

'Well, perhaps I should have said, did it seem to you in character?'

'Yes, I think so. Why does it matter?'

'Only that she claims to have taken Barry Jones on without any references and to know nothing about him beyond what he told her, that he had once been a school teacher and had had a nervous breakdown. I just wondered if it strikes you that that's the sort of thing she'd be likely to do.'

'I think it probably is.'

'I see.' He brought the tips of his fingers together. 'Now will you tell me, did you take the Vauxhall out any time yesterday evening or this morning?'

'I took it out yesterday morning, but not since then.'

'Do you know if anyone else took it out?'

'I don't think so.'

'But the garage doors are open this morning.'

'They were hardly ever closed.'

He nodded thoughtfully. 'Now, talking of your sister, I'd like to know if you happen to have made the acquaintance of a young photographer in the town called David Kaye.'

'Yes,' Alison said, 'I had a long talk with him yesterday morning.'

'How did that come about? Had he got in touch with your family?'

'No, he actually mistook me for my sister in the street and called out at me. Then when he realized he'd blundered, he turned and bolted. But I asked Mrs Rumbold, the daily who works for the Eckersalls, if she could tell me who he probably was and she said he sounded like a young man Sally had been going about with and she told me where to find him. So I went to his studio in the High Street and we had this talk I mentioned.'

'You know we've had some contact with that young man,' Mr Ditteridge said. 'In fact, it was he who told us of your sister's disappearance.'

'And when you couldn't find any proof he'd murdered her, you dropped the matter.'

'Not exactly, no.' Mr Ditteridge gave her one of his shrewdly observant glances. 'You needn't be afraid the file's been closed, Mrs Goodrich. The search has gone on, but so far we've found no trace of her. However, Jones's murder may open up a new line of inquiry.'

'Do you mean you think David Kaye killed Jones? Do you think David found some connection between Jones and Sally and came here and killed in revenge?'

'Now, now, Mrs Goodrich.' Mr Ditteridge looked disapproving. 'You're going much too fast for us. It doesn't pay, you know. Take things slowly, check everything as you go, that's the best advice I can give you. I understand your concern for your sister and as you had the suspicions you did of the Eckersalls, may I say it was courageous of you to put your head, so to speak, in the lion's mouth. All the same, we don't want to start jumping to conclusions before we've any evidence, do we? But I'll tell you one little bit of evidence we've got and I'll be interested in what you think of it. There's a bottle of red hair-dye in Jones's flat and that moustache of his was false.'

'So he was disguised.' Alison found that she was not really surprised.

'Unquestionably.'

'Well . . .' She hesitated. 'I always felt he wasn't what he made himself out to be. For instance, he was always talking about how mad he was, how he might wake up any morning thinking he was God and things like that, but I felt quite sure he was really as sane as the rest of us.'

'What do you think Mr and Mrs Eckersall thought about him?'

'I really don't know.'

'You never noticed anything – call it unusual – in their relationship with him?'

'I don't think I can remember even seeing them talking to him.'

'Is that so?' He said it slowly, frowning, as if he found something strange in what she had said. 'Did it strike you that that might have been deliberate?'

'Why should it be? Oh . . .!' She had understood where his questions were leading. 'You were wondering if they were helping to hide him here, if they knew much more about him than they wanted to let on and were being careful not to let anyone have the chance to see how well they knew each other.'

'Well, what do you think about that?'

'I don't know,' she said. 'He was a very reserved kind of person. He didn't seem to welcome human contact much. He liked to be left alone.'

'Understandably, if he was in hiding. So you never saw him with any of the household.'

'No, but . . .'

'Yes?'

'Oh, I suppose I ought to tell you. I didn't see them together, but yesterday morning I got up early and I was at my window and I saw Miss Pullen come running back to the house from his flat.'

'It was your impression that they'd spent the night together?'

'I can't be sure of it, but – yes.'

'Ah,' Mr Ditteridge said and took a long look at her

face, as if he were looking there for signs of spite or jealousy. 'Do you think Mr and Mrs Eckersall were aware of the association?'

'I don't know.'

'And of course you've no knowledge yourself when it began.'

'Are you wondering if she could have introduced him here, whoever he was?'

'There you go again, much too fast for me! All the same, it's a question that naturally springs to mind. Now about the car that was seen here in the night by Miss Fisk. Mrs Eckersall told us about it and naturally we shall be questioning Miss Fisk herself concerning it, but I'd like to know if you saw it.'

'No.'

'That's a pity. I was hoping you might be able to tell us when it arrived. If it arrived at all. I'm afraid there's a possibility that Miss Fisk imagined the car. I know the lady.' He gave a depressed kind of smile. 'I don't welcome the thought of putting her in the witness-box.' He stood up. He was dismissing her. 'I think that's all for the present, unless you can think of something you feel we ought to know.'

Alison stood up too. 'I don't think so. But I'd like to telephone my brother. Do you mind if I do that?'

'Not in the least. But I think you'd be wise not to talk of what's happened to anyone you can help. The Press, for instance.'

'I hadn't thought of doing such a thing.'

'Good. And if you think of anything that might help, don't hesitate to come to me, even if whatever it is seems very trivial.'

'But about my sister . . .'

'Yes?'

'You've *no* trace of her? You say you haven't given up

looking for her, but you've found out *nothing*?'

She saw a curious flicker in his eyes. It looked almost as if there were something that he wanted to say to her. Then he blotted that faint trace of expression from his face.

'I did say Jones's murder may open up a new line of inquiry,' he said. 'Identifying him may tell us quite a lot, and I've a feeling that that isn't going to be too difficult. But let me warn you about one thing.' He went to the door and held it open for her. 'Even if we find out what's happened, don't start taking for granted that it's going to be good news. I promise to tell you anything we find out about her, but – I don't like to say this – you may wish you hadn't heard it.'

She lingered in the doorway. 'I think you do know something.'

He shook his head. 'If I'd your habit of jumping ahead when I've no evidence I trust, I might say yes, but that wouldn't be fair to you, or to her, or to anybody. Let's wait and see what we think when we've identified Jones. Now would you mind asking Miss Pullen to come to see me?'

CHAPTER VIII

JUNE PULLEN and Mr Eckersall were in the drawing-room. From the sound of their low voices, Alison thought that they were quarrelling.

She was right. Just before going into the room she heard June say, 'All the same, I know what I know. You've been feeling mad with jealousy of him.'

'Are you saying you believe I did it?' Mr Eckersall's voice went high and querulous. 'The girl's crazy. The man might have been some use to me alive. Dead, he's just one hell of a danger.'

He sounded as if he were speaking to a third person in the room, but when Alison went in she found only him and June there. Mrs Eckersall was in the garden, watching the progress of an ambulance up the muddy drive. There were several policemen in the garden too, poking about here and there among the shrubs and flowers. Looking for the weapon, Alison supposed. The gun.

Unless it was for something else.

But if what they were looking for was a sign that six feet of earth had been disturbed recently, there was not much hope of finding it after last night's torrent of rain. Or was that the wrong way about? Might not the rain have washed away enough surface earth to reveal secrets?

Alison stood still, staring at the men, frightened by her own thoughts, until Mr Eckersall, turning on her, said sharply, 'Well?'

She gave a start and said, 'I'm sorry. I was asked by Mr Ditteridge to say that he'd like to speak to Miss Pullen.'

'To this fool girl?' He turned on June, took her by the

shoulders and shook her. 'You listen to me, June. None of the sort of nonsense now you've just been talking to me. Stick to facts and don't go in for a lot of fancy embroidery.'

'It's all right, I know what to say to him.' She jerked away from him, her pretty face sullen and pinched. 'But don't try to scare me, or I may tell him more of the truth than you'd like.'

'For God's sake, I'm not trying to scare you, I'm only telling you not to make a fool of yourself,' he said.

She gave a mocking little smile and went out.

Mr Eckersall came to Alison and put an arm round her waist. He was one of the men who can hardly talk to a woman without touching her.

'Worrying about that talk we had last night?' he asked. 'No need to, my dear. We're good friends, aren't we? Or d'you think I'm a murderer, as that miserable little bitch does? I thought she was fond of me, and then she practically calls me a murderer to my face. I told her, Barry alive was some use to me. He was a damn good gardener. We haven't a hope of getting another like him. But what good is he to me dead?'

It was a crude attempt to cover up what he was afraid that Alison had heard as she came into the room. Only it did not account for his having called the dead Barry Jones a danger to him.

'There's Mrs Rumbold arriving,' she said as she saw the stout woman bicycling up the drive in the wake of the ambulance. 'I thought she didn't come on Sundays.'

'She doesn't,' he said. 'But bad news travels fast and she's one of the most damned inquisitive females I've ever met. Now how d'you feel about making me a plate of bacon and eggs? I've missed my breakfast and my guts are rumbling with hunger. Or aren't you our cook any more? Kind of a peculiar relationship we've got ourselves into, isn't it? But if it's all right with you to carry on as before

– you know what I mean, as if we'd never had that talk last night – that would suit us all fine. The police aren't going to let you go away for some time anyhow.'

'I'll gladly go on doing the cooking,' Alison said, thinking that it would be far better to have something to do than to sit about with nothing in her mind but the kind of thoughts that had been coming into it too often recently.

She was trying to move out of his embrace when he added, 'And you won't season my eggs with too much rat poison, will you, even if you think I'm a rat – ha, ha!' He really said ha, ha, pantomiming a sinister laugh. 'After all, one of us around here may be a murderer and for all we know, it's you. Could be my dear wife, of course, or could even be me. Perhaps dear little June is right and I did it, though I don't remember a thing about it. Got up and walked in my sleep and went and shot poor old Barry. Well, well, pardon my bad jokes and I'll be grateful for life for those bacon and eggs.'

He let her go and she went quickly along the passage to the kitchen.

More than anything else just then she wanted to talk to Geoffrey, but the police were in the study where one telephone extension was, Mr Eckersall was in the drawing-room, where there was another, and as Alison reached the kitchen, where there was a third, Mrs Rumbold came puffing in. So talking to Geoffrey would have to wait.

As Alison went to the refrigerator for the bacon and eggs for Mr Eckersall's breakfast, Mrs Rumbold plumped herself down on a chair and began massaging her knees. She must have cycled more speedily than usual and be suffering for it now. As usual, she had on a good deal of make-up, but it showed signs of having been put on in a great hurry. The very bright pink lipstick that she favoured was smudged along the edges. Under her thick, drooping eyelids, touched up with green, her little eyes gleamed with excitement.

'How you can look so calm!' she exclaimed. 'You're all right, are you, dear? It isn't shock, you really feel all right? It's wonderful, keeping your head like that. Of course, Sunday isn't my day for coming, but I said to Joe when I heard, you never know, I said, perhaps I can help. I wouldn't want to let my friends down if there's any way I can help when they're in trouble. That's how I think of Mr and Mrs Eckersall, I said, they're my friends, and I hope that's how they think of me. I'm sure they know they can count on me any time, whether it's sickness or something worse like this.'

'How did you hear what happened?' Alison asked, taking a frying-pan out of a cupboard.

'The milkman told me,' Mrs Rumbold answered. 'He was coming here to deliver the milk as usual, but a police-man stopped him and said he was to keep out, there'd been murder done, and that was all he knew, and when he told me I thought it's that June Pullen, sure to be. But I had a word just now with Mr Hankinson out there – he's one of the constables and he used to live with his mum and dad next door but one to Joe and me till he went into the police and got married and got one of the police houses – and he told me it was Barry. You know, I always thought there was something strange about that man and I'd never have been surprised if it had been suicide, people who've had what they call nervous break-downs being apt to find life's a bit too much for them, but murder . . .' She shook her head.

'Why did you think it was June?' Alison asked, breaking eggs into the frying-pan.

'Now don't pretend, dear,' Mrs Rumbold said. 'The family's been down here since Friday. Don't tell me you haven't seen what's going on.'

'Well, suppose I have, why should it have led to murder? That's going rather far, isn't it?'

'Ah, but you never know what people will do when they've had a bit too much to drink. They all drink too much here, let's face it. I can tell by the bottles they put out in the dustbin. I've often said to Mrs Eckersall, "You all drink more than's right, dear," I said, "it isn't going to do you any good, specially at your age when you shouldn't hardly need it. It's different at my age," I said, "you need something sometimes when your back's bothering you or you're just tired out, you don't know why. But all the same, all I have is my Guinness at night, or sometimes a brandy puff, like I told you. But if you aren't careful, dear, it'll grow on you," I said, "and then you don't know what'll happen to your character."'

'And what did Mrs Eckersall say to that?'

'Oh, she laughed. That's what I like about her, you can say what you like to her. She said, "Oh, I lost my character long ago, Mrs Rumbold, a little whisky won't do me any harm." "But I'm serious," I said, "it doesn't come on all at once, but ten years from now you'll wish you'd listened to me." And I wish she *had* listened to me, because now look what's happened.'

'You're saying Mrs Eckersall killed Barry Jones in a fit of drunken fury?' Alison said.

Mrs Eckersall was the one person in the household of whom she had no suspicions. For why should a woman murder a man who was so successfully taking her husband's mistress away from him?

'No, no, I'm not talking about Barry at all,' Mrs Rumbold said. 'I'm talking about that June Pullen.'

Alison tried in vain to follow her reasoning. 'But nobody's murdered June.'

'No, but *if* they had . . .' Mrs Rumbold gave a rather regretful sigh. Plainly from her point of view the girl would have been no loss. 'Ah dear, my knees are terrible this morning. It's the damp. And I didn't even get wet last night to speak of. Joe and me got home from the Good Intent before the storm really started. A terrible storm, wasn't it? My friend, Mrs Jellaby, who lives across the road from us and works mornings for Colonel Mayberry, stayed on and she said she saw a ball of fire come in at the lounge door and go twice round the room and out of the window. She says she doesn't know when she's been so frightened.'

Alison was so used to thinking of Colonel Mayberry as a ginger tom cat that for a moment she was puzzled why he should need the services of a Mrs Jellaby. Then she remembered that the Fisk sisters, not knowing the animal's real name, called it after its owner.

'Had Mrs Jellaby been drinking brandy puffs?' she asked.

'No, just tomato juice,' Mrs Rumbold answered. 'Not even a drop of gin in it. She comes to the Good Intent for the company. That's why she goes out to work too, she doesn't need the money. Her Fred was killed in an accident at the works and she got very good compensation. But she likes to have someone to talk to and Colonel Mayberry's a very nice friendly man, even if the Miss Fisks have got it in for him. Is it true, dear, that those two old women discovered the body?'

Alison slid the bacon and eggs on to a plate.

'It was they who came here and told me about it,' she said. 'I suppose it's possible that someone else found it before them.'

'And said nothing about it? My goodness!'

'Well, there's a story about a car that was here in the night.'

'A car? Would that have been the murderer's car?'

Mrs Rumbold ran the tip of her tongue excitedly along her shiny pink lips. 'I'll tell you what I think – '

'Just a minute,' Alison said. 'I must take this in to Mr Eckersall.'

She took his breakfast to the dining-room and went to the drawing-room to tell him that it was waiting for him.

She found Mrs Eckersall, June Pullen and Mr Ditteridge there too. At the moment when Alison went in they were all silent and the atmosphere was dense with hostility. Mr Eckersall had his chin thrust forward as if he had just delivered some kind of ultimatum. His soft jowls were quivering slightly. Mrs Eckersall was looking extraordinarily tired, with her eyes staring even more stonily than usual out of her white face. June Pullen looked for once as if she were trying to make herself as inconspicuous as possible. The superintendent's face showed the irritability of boredom, as if this were a situation he had encountered only too often before.

'Very well, if you insist, I'll apply for a search warrant,' he said. 'But it'll merely cause delay. In the end your house and garden will be searched for the weapon. If you would let my men begin the search now, it might help very greatly, if only by eliminating the possibility that the gun's been hidden here.'

'Oh, go ahead, go ahead,' Mrs Eckersall said impatiently. 'I can't stand all this talk. Go ahead, Mr Ditteridge. Don't listen to my husband.'

'I'm only standing on my rights,' Mr Eckersall said sulkily. 'For one thing, we're sure the murderer came and went in that car the Fisks saw and took the gun away with him. Why aren't you looking for the car instead of bothering us?'

'I think perhaps we've found it,' Mr Ditteridge answered.

'Found it – already? You amaze me!' Mr Eckersall

made it sound as if he were sure the superintendent was lying to him.

'Yes, as you'll remember, I asked each of you if you'd taken the Vauxhall out of the garage either last night or this morning,' Mr Ditteridge said, 'and you all said no. But someone took it out after the storm started. There are muddy tyre tracks on the floor of the garage. None going out, but a very clear set going in. So someone took that car out after your drive got muddy in the rain. Someone must have paused outside the garage long enough for the car to have been seen in a flash of lightning, although, its being by Miss Fisk, she didn't recognize the car.'

At that point Alison interrupted, 'Mr Eckersall, your breakfast's waiting in the dining-room.'

For a moment she thought that he was going to swear at her for being such a fool as to mention something as unimportant as breakfast at a time like this, but then he seemed suddenly to think that there was something to be said for escaping from the scene here. Beaming at her, he patted her shoulder, said, 'Thank you, thank you, now I'll survive,' and plunged out of the drawing-room. Alison turned and went back to the kitchen.

'Mrs Rumbold, I've got something on my mind,' she said, 'and I'd be very grateful if you'd help clear it up for me. You've worked here for some time, haven't you?'

'Why yes, dear, ever since they moved in,' Mrs Rumbold answered. 'That's about six months ago. Why d'you want to know?'

'Well, you know the house very well, don't you?'

'I suppose I do.'

'You know that walnut bureau in the study.'

'Yes, of course. I give it a good polishing every week. Handsome, I've always thought it.'

'I just wondered if it was always locked or only sometimes,' Alison said.

Mrs Rumbold had made herself a cup of instant coffee. Stirring sugar into it, she remarked, 'Funny you should say that. I often wondered about it myself. Everything in the house wide open, sometimes even a box of Mrs Eckersall's left behind with valuable jewellery in it, but just the top of that bureau always kept locked. Important papers, I thought. Some people are very fussy about their papers. I once worked for a gentleman who was writing a book and he used to scatter papers all over the floor of his room and he told me I was never to touch any of them unless they were actually in the waste-paper basket. And once I did. I made a neat pile of a few of them so that I could get round with my vacuum cleaner and I thought, they're such a mess, he'll never notice. And the first thing he said when he went into the room was, "Someone's been buggering my papers about." Pardon the language, but it's what he said, dear. So I know papers are very important to some gentlemen, and I said to myself, it stands to reason that's what's in the bureau, papers to do with Mr Eckersall's business. Don't you think that's what it must be?'

'Perhaps,' Alison said. 'But there's nothing in it now.'

'You mean it's open?' Mrs Rumbold looked very surprised. She must often have tried to open that flap, Alison thought, and taken her own curiosity so much for granted that it never occurred to her to try to conceal it.

'It was open when I took the police in there this morning,' Alison said.

'And when you saw it open, it was empty?' Mrs Rumbold said wonderingly. 'Well, isn't that strange? Keeping an empty desk locked up – fancy! Though of course someone could have come in during the night and stolen whatever was in it, most likely the same person who killed poor Barry. What d'you think about that?'

'It seems quite possible.'

Mrs Rumbold nodded thoughtfully. 'Yes, that'll be what happened. And I think I could tell you who it was. After all, who knows enough about Mr Eckersall's business to know what was in that desk?'

'You're talking about June Pullen again?'

Mrs Rumbold nodded once more with brooding significance.

Alison thought of the figure that she had seen running along the terrace in the early morning of the day before, her rosy face, her radiance, her skip of sheer happiness as she made for the porch.

'I don't think I can see her murdering Barry Jones,' she said.

'Not even if he came in and caught her? Took the papers she wanted from her? Threatened her with telling Mr Eckersall?'

'No. Anyway, not for any reason like that.'

Mrs Rumbold gave Alison a deep, questioning look, as if she were wondering how she came by such certainty.

At that moment the front-door bell rang.

Alison went to answer it. David Kaye stood in the porch. She saw at once that she would not have to tell him much about what had happened, for there was a look of tension and anxiety on his face which showed that he knew most of it already. His Volkswagen was in the road just beyond the gates of the drive.

'Why have you come?' she asked. 'There's nothing you can do here.'

'I came to see if you were all right,' he answered. 'Can you believe it, the first thing the police did when they found out about the murder was to send someone out to my caravan to ask me for my alibi for last night? Just wait and see, they're going to pin this on me if they can. They still think I murdered Sally and now they think

I killed Jones because he found out something about it and was blackmailing me, or just threatening to turn me in. Actually I've never even spoken to the man. But when the police went away I thought you'd have to tell them the truth about yourself and what you were doing here and that perhaps I could help you in some way. I don't suppose I can, but I thought – oh, I just thought it might help somehow to have me around. I'll go away if you'd sooner I did.'

'No, stay,' she said. 'It was nice of you to come. But what did you tell them about your alibi?'

'You don't want to talk to me till you know if I've got one, is that it?'

'No, of course not. I was just hoping for your own sake that you had.'

'You wouldn't expect me to be as lucky as that!'

'You're like the rest of us here then,' she said. 'So far as I know, nobody's got one. Come in and have some coffee.'

She took him to the kitchen.

He and Mrs Rumbold greeted one another with the casual nods of old acquaintances. Mrs Rumbold made him a cup of instant coffee.

Sitting down at the table, he said, 'As a matter of fact, I've an alibi for the early part of the evening. I had some steak and chips with some chaps I know in the Seven Bells and we stayed on talking till closing time. The rain was bucketing down when we left. But I spent the rest of the evening in the caravan, reading. The car was beside it. But it's in a fairly lonely place on a farmer's bit of land and unless he happened to notice the car there'll be no one to say I was there.'

So it was not impossible that it was David's car that the Fisk sisters had seen outside the garage, even if for some unknown reason someone from the house had driven the

Vauxhall out of it and back again during the night or
the early morning.

She began to think about the garage and the muddy
tyre tracks that she had not noticed when she passed it
with the Fisks, going to Barry Jones's flat. But she had
noticed something else. There had been something about
the garage of more interest to her than the tracks,
although for the moment she could not think what it
was. Then suddenly she remembered.

David was still talking, but she was not listening. He
noticed it and said, 'What is it, Alison? I think I'm in the
way. I'd better go.'

'No, it's just that I've thought of something I want to
tell Mr Ditteridge. Something awfully trivial. But he said
I was to tell him anything that might be useful, however
trivial it was.'

'Shall I come with you?'

'Yes, do. This thing may mean more to you than it
does to me.'

'I'll come too,' Mrs Rumbold stated, getting to her
feet. 'I'd like to be useful.'

Alison did not see how the stout woman possibly could
be useful, but she was not likely to do any harm and it
would be difficult to stop her coming if that was what she
had made up her mind to do. The three of them went
looking for Mr Ditteridge.

They found him in the drawing-room, superintending
a search of the room that was being made by two constables. Neither of the Eckersalls was there. As the three
entered, one of the constables had just lifted the flowers
that Alison had arranged on Friday out of their vase and
was peering down into it to see, she supposed, if the gun
had been dropped into the water under the flowers.

Apparently there was nothing there, for he stuck the
flowers back into the vase, unfortunately so clumsily

that they stood up straight in a tight bunch which she could hardly bear to leave as it was. However, she had not come there to give the police force lessons in flower arrangement.

'Mr Ditteridge, I want to tell you about something I noticed this morning,' she said. 'It was in the garage – just a puddle of water under the nozzle of the hose. That green plastic hose that's attached to a standpipe in the garage and hung up in coils on a hook on the wall. Well, you know what happens when you've been using a hose and then you turn the tap off. If the nozzle's hanging down, the hose goes on dripping for a bit. So that's where the puddle came from. But why should anyone have been using a hose yesterday? Barry Jones said in the morning a storm was coming, so he wouldn't have wasted his time watering the garden, and who else would have had any reason for using it?'

Mr Ditteridge looked blank. She thought that she had not made her point clear or else that he thought it positively too trivial to have been worth mentioning to him. But it turned out that he was merely thinking it over.

'I noticed that puddle,' he said. 'I didn't pay much attention to it. I thought it probably had something to do with cleaning the Lagonda. That had obviously been done since it was driven down on Friday. It hasn't a speck of dust on it.'

'Barry Jones cleaned it yesterday morning,' Alison said. 'He was giving it a polish when I took the Vauxhall out to go shopping, and that was fairly early in the morning. So if he'd hosed the Lagonda down first, that puddle would have had around twenty-four hours to dry up. On a day as warm as yesterday, don't you think it would have done that?'

The superintendent tugged at his chin, frowning at her. Behind him the two constables were taking all the books out of a bookcase, then, finding nothing, putting them back.

'Have you some idea about that puddle, Mrs Goodrich?' he asked. 'I'm grateful to you for pointing it out to me, mind, but at the moment it doesn't mean anything to me.'

'It doesn't mean anything to me,' she said. 'It was just something I noticed.'

'I've got an idea about it,' David said.

Alison and Mr Ditteridge both looked at him.

'Am I right,' he said, 'that someone saw a car standing in the drive some time during the storm last night and that no one knows just when it arrived or left? That's what the man who came to ask me for my alibi told me.'

'Yes, that's more or less right,' Mr Ditteridge said.

'Only more or less?'

'Well, there's some evidence that the Vauxhall was taken out during the night. That may have been the car that Miss Fisk saw.'

'In that case my idea's no good,' David said. 'I won't bother you with it.'

'There may have been another car, however.'

'Do you mean that?'

'Oh yes, there may have been half a dozen cars, for all we know. What's your idea, Mr Kaye?'

'It's just this. Suppose a car arrived here before the rain began, a car belonging to someone coming to see Jones. And suppose it stayed until after the rain stopped. I'm not saying that whoever came in it did the murder. I'm only talking about the car. Well, when it drove off there'd have been a dry patch where it had stood, wouldn't there? Even this morning, with the ground still as wet as it is, the patch would have shown. And suppose someone, either the man who came in the car, or even Jones himself, wanted to conceal the fact that the car had been here, a few minutes' work with the hose would have blotted out that dry patch. Well, that's all. It isn't much of an idea, I know, but you might just give it some thought.'

Mr Ditteridge smiled wryly. 'Enough thought to notice you've suggested an excellent alibi for yourself, Mr Kaye? Was that your reason for coming here this morning – to make sure this idea occurred to us?'

'I don't understand,' David said.

'Oh, come, you've an alibi, haven't you, for the early part of the evening? You were with friends in the Seven Bells and it was raining hard already by the time you left. But this car you're talking about must have got here, as you've just said yourself, before the rain began, or there'd have been no dry patch under it. So it couldn't have been yours. Very neat and very subtle, or else perhaps a little bit too simple. I wonder which it is.'

'Now, listen, Mr Ditteridge!' Mrs Rumbold exploded. 'I won't have anyone calling David simple! I've known him most of his life and there's never been anything wrong with his brains. A very bright little boy, that's what he always was. Simple, indeed! It's an insult.'

David began to laugh. 'It's all right, Mrs Rumbold, the superintendent doesn't mean what you think he does. I rather wish he did. People forgive nearly everything if one's a bit defective. One can steal and murder and rape and get away with a little sentence of doing arts and crafts. All the same, Mr Ditteridge, I'm not as subtle as you think. I wasn't thinking about my alibi at all, but just that I'd come up with rather a nice theory. I've another one, if you'd like to hear it.'

'Go ahead, Mr Kaye.'

'Well, it's just that someone used that hose to douse Jones, to make it look as if he'd been killed before the rain stopped. Someone with an alibi for the later part of the night. I've got it right, haven't I? Your chap who ques-

tioned me told me that Jones's clothes were wet and it
had rained into his room, and he only seemed to be
interested in what I was doing until the end of the storm.'

'It looks as if you got more information out of him than
he did out of you,' Mr Ditteridge said. 'I'll have to speak
to him. But I like this theory of yours better than the
other one. The only trouble about it is that I can't find
anyone who has an alibi for any time of the night, from
about eleven o'clock on. Not one of the people I've
questioned so far would benefit by getting us to believe
that the murder happened before the storm stopped.
But there's one thing we know and that is that Jones had
a visitor last night. We don't know if he, or perhaps she,
arrived in the car Miss Fisk saw and as early as you sug-
gest, but there's a bottle of whisky with two glasses on a
table in Jones's room and there are nice clear fingerprints
on the glasses. So I'm shortly going to be asking you all
to allow yourselves to have your fingerprints taken. You
can refuse, if you want to, but you can see how helpful
it'll be if you cooperate. How about letting us begin with
you, Mr Kaye?'

'Glad to,' David said cheerfully.

Mrs Rumbold was inclined to object on the grounds
that it meant getting a lot of nasty muck on her fingers,
but one of the constables said, 'It's all right, missus, we'll
clean you up nicely,' and on the superintendent's orders,
he went to fetch the necessary gear.

Alison thought that she knew whose the fingerprints on
one of the glasses would turn out to be, but she was wrong.
They were not June Pullen's. She was also wrong in
expecting that Mr Eckersall would make a fuss at being
asked to let his prints be taken. Rather to her surprise,
nobody made a fuss. The whole affair went off very
quietly, as quietly as the search of the house and garden
was now proceeding, and presently Mr Ditteridge told

them all that it was quite certain that the prints on the glass that Jones had not used had not been made by anyone in the house. He left soon afterwards to go and talk to the Fisks, but the search for the gun went on for most of the day.

Alison opened some tins and produced a lunch of sorts, but no one had any appetite. David Kaye would not stay for lunch and Mrs Rumbold also left for home. The Eckersalls wanted several rounds of drinks before they would settle down to eat and insisted on Alison joining them, although when the three of them and June Pullen were sitting in the drawing-room no one had anything special to say. Alison still itched to telephone Geoffrey, yet though all of them seemed lost in their private thoughts, they seemed unwilling to let her out of their sight. She had a feeling of something building up, like the storm of the evening before, some conflict between them that would shortly explode in some violent way. Yet nothing happened.

Nothing, at least, until a young constable looked into the room, holding June's fluffy pink bedroom slippers.

As soon as she saw them her face turned livid and she screeched at him, 'What are you doing with those?'

He asked, 'Are they yours, Miss Pullen?'

'They are and you just put them back where you found them!' she cried. 'What are you doing with them?'

'I'm afraid I'll have to take them away,' he said. 'There's some substance on them that Mr Ditteridge may wish to have analysed.'

'Some substance?' Her voice was still wild. 'What are you trying to say – that it's blood?'

'Not blood, no, it's not the colour,' he said. 'But it's tacky like. More like treacle. And there are traces of treacle on the floor in Jones's flat.'

Mrs Eckersall began to laugh. 'Treacle! Oh, June, what a silly little girl you are!'

'But he can't simply take my slippers like that, can he?'
June said, subsiding a little, though still with a good deal
of defiance. '*Can* he?' she repeated, turning to Mr Eckersall.

'God knows,' he muttered. 'When I want to stand up
for my rights I'm told I'm a fool. But I'd let him take the
damn things if I were you. Can't do any harm. Treacle!'
His face suddenly lit up and he gave a little giggle. He
seemed to have arrived already at his usual state of semi-
drunkenness. 'Why pretend, darling? We all know how
you got that on your shoes.'

'But I never – I didn't – I don't know how it happened.'

While she was protesting the policeman quietly with-
drew, taking the slippers with him.

Mr Eckersall grinned at June with a certain cruelty.

'You know all right,' he said. 'Those mad women from
next door smeared the stuff all over the ground right up
to the bottom of Barry's steps. But we're all friends here,
so as I said, why pretend? Far better if we all have the
same story about everything. We'll stick by you to the
end, won't we, Louise?'

'But I didn't go up there in the night,' June said, almost
crying. 'Earlier in the evening – well, all right, yes, I did,
but not for long and it was long before the Fisks saw that
car. Don't you believe me?'

'I don't see that it matters what we believe,' Mrs
Eckersall said. 'It isn't a crime to get treacle on your
shoes. It isn't even a crime to have an affair with the
gardener. Now let's go and eat that lunch that's waiting
for us.'

She finished her whisky at a gulp and went to the dining-
room.

Alison thought that she would telephone Geoffrey when
she had cleared away the lunch, but by then the police
were searching the kitchen, so she still could not use the

extension. She did not see when the body of Barry Jones was taken away in the ambulance, but at last all the police departed. It was about five o'clock when she managed to make her telephone call.

Katrina answered and before Alison could tell her anything said that she had been waiting all day for the call, because she had felt certain ever since she had woken up that morning that something terrible had happened.

When Alison said that murder had happened, Katrina said, 'Oh God, Alison, I knew it – I really knew it!' But Katrina was so often sure that she knew when something terrible, or wonderful, or merely extraordinary had happened or was about to happen, that she could hardly fail to be right now and then. All the same, she could be eerily convincing sometimes.

Alison asked her to fetch Geoffrey and when he came to the telephone she told him the story of the day. She told him too how she had been identified as Sally's sister and that if it had not been for the murder she would have returned to London that morning.

'And you've found out nothing about Sally?' he said.

'Nothing at all.'

'Yet you can't come home?'

'I don't think I can yet.'

'Katrina keeps saying she's sure you ought to. I wish you would too.'

'I think possibly it's just become important for me to stay. I think things may be going to come out that may tell us something we want to know.'

'Yes, but . . .' He paused. 'Well, at least take care. Lock your door at night. Avoid lonely places. Don't talk to strange men. And I'll come down and join you if they'll let me off at the office for a few days. That might be the best thing to do.'

'Perhaps it would.'

'I'll see what I can do about it.'

They rang off.

Alison began trying to recollect what she had intended
to give the Eckersalls for dinner that evening and remembered that she had bought a piece of sirloin the day before.
But it seemed much too much trouble to cook it at the end
of such a day, so she gave them scrambled eggs and cheese
and chose to eat hers alone in the kitchen. As if they
had recognized that she was no longer really the cook,
June helped her to clear away after the meal, but as soon
as Alison had set the dishwasher going, she turned and
ran up to her room. A few minutes later Alison followed
her up to hers.

Next morning about ten o'clock Mr Ditteridge reappeared with the large sergeant and two or three other
men and the search for the gun was resumed. A good deal
of it was simply a repetition of what had been done the
day before. The morning was a golden one. The blue of
the sky was deep and shining and the grass of the lawn,
beloved of Barry Jones, almost glittered. Alison wondered
what June had really felt about him. She showed no
signs of grief or stress, but looked as if she had had a good
night's sleep and was looking forward in a mood of cheerful relaxation to the day before her. The same could not be
said of the Eckersalls. Both their faces had a tinge of
greyness, which suggested that they had not slept. At the
same time they had an air of having drawn much closer
together than Alison had ever seen them before. Possibly,
she thought, it was only that they furtively shared some
secret which it was to the advantage of both of them to
keep, but something had lessened the antagonism that
they usually showed to each other. In their unfamiliar
unity they were almost like a happily married couple.

Upstairs Mrs Rumbold was busy with the vacuum
cleaner, but as soon as she saw the police arrive she

switched it off and came hurrying downstairs, eager not to miss anything. This brought Mrs Eckersall out of her mood of apparent quiet and her voice shook as she exploded, 'Get back to your job and stop pushing your nose into our affairs! If the police want you they'll send for you, but till then stop watching us, and eavesdropping on us, and creeping round us!'

It was the first time that Alison had seen the temper that she had heard of.

'Now, Louise – ' her husband began placatingly, but she went on shouting, 'I can't stand being watched! If the damned woman goes on with it she can quit. I won't be spied on!'

'There now, what did I tell you?' Mrs Rumbold said, placidly appearing to take no offence. 'Got a head this morning, have you? I wonder how late you stayed up last night, drinking. Where would you be if I did quit, I'd like to know.'

However, she went upstairs and the humming of the vacuum cleaner started up again.

Almost at once Mrs Eckersall looked sorry for having flared up as she had and turned towards the stairs, as if she were about to go up to apologize to Mrs Rumbold. But just then the doorbell rang and she went to the door to let in Mr Ditteridge.

After all, he wanted to speak to Mrs Rumbold as well as to the others in the house, so Alison fetched her downstairs again and they all assembled in the drawing-room, obviously to listen to some grave announcement. There was something about Mr Ditteridge's face this morning that Alison did not like the look of. She realized something about him that she had hardly noticed the day before when he was being so mild and courteous to everybody, and that was that as an antagonist he would be a very formidable man. And this morning he had come here as an antagonist. She wondered of whom, and in spite of her own relatively easy conscience, felt a flicker of irrational fear. For why shouldn't it be of herself? Some of her actions during the last few days must have struck him as decidedly suspicious and he did not happen to share her positive knowledge that she had not killed Barry Jones.

But when he began to speak in a quiet, level voice, it was at Mr Eckersall that he looked.

'I've come to tell you that we've identified Barry Jones,' he said. 'His name was not Barry Jones. It was Arthur Small. Does that mean anything to you? I was fairly sure of it yesterday, but I didn't want to say anything about it till we'd checked his fingerprints. Three years ago Arthur Small was given ten years for robbery with violence. Not his first sentence by any means. He and an accomplice robbed a bank of two hundred thousand pounds. One of the bank tellers who tried to give the alarm was brutally beaten and has never wholly recovered. The accomplice got away with the money and Small never told us who he was. We were fairly sure we knew, but the man we suspected had an alibi that we couldn't break. Then three weeks ago Small escaped from prison. He had help from outside, we know that, and he totally vanished. But his photograph has been shown on television on a number of occasions, and if you ever watch the news I doubt if you can have failed to see it. Well, that's the man you've employed here as a gardener. The school you told me he was employed by before he had his mental breakdown never existed. Nor, I think, did the breakdown. And the visitor he had last night, whose fingerprints are on the glass in Small's room, belong to a man called Jack Cassell, who's the man we believe did the bank job with him. We picked him up last night and when he heard murder was involved he

talked fairly freely. His story about last night is that he
came here by bus before the storm began, walking the
last bit of the way, that he and Small talked for some time
and had some drinks together, then because the rain had
begun Small got the Vauxhall out and drove Cassell to
the station. That he did that has been corroborated by a
porter who saw the two of them there. But Cassell also
says, Mr Eckersall, that you knew quite well all along
that you've been harbouring a criminal – '

Alison could not wait any longer. It had been hard
enough for her to let him talk for as long as she had. She
had to break in.

'But it's obvious now what happened to Sally! She was
here when Arthur Small arrived. Isn't she supposed to
have left just before he was taken on? But the truth must
be that she was still here and she'd seen him on television
and she recognized him. And so – and so I think he killed
her. Isn't that what happened?'

Mr Ditteridge turned his grave glance to her.

'Didn't I tell you that Jones's murder might open up a
new line of inquiry?' he said. 'I also promised to tell
you anything we found out, but said that when we did,
you might wish we hadn't.'

CHAPTER IX

'No!' Mrs Eckersall said harshly and positively. 'That was not how it happened.'

'Louise,' her husband said warningly. 'You don't have to say anything.'

'There are some things it's just as well to say,' she answered.

'Not now.'

'Yes, now. Why not?'

All of them except Mr Ditteridge, who had taken up a position in front of the empty fireplace, were still standing in a knot just inside the door. Mrs Eckersall walked forward, dropped on to a sofa and gave some attention to making herself comfortable.

'Why not, since we can't help it that a lot of things are going to come out?' she said almost placidly. 'But I don't see why we should let ourselves be labelled as accomplices to a murder. Arthur Small did not murder your sister, Alison. I think he might have tried to if we'd let him, but we stopped it.'

Mr Eckersall gave a deep sigh, crossed the room and sat down beside his wife. There was a look of defeat about him.

'All right, go on,' he said.

'It's true that Sally walked in on us and recognized Small,' Mrs Eckersall said. 'He'd come to us in London and we didn't know what to do with him but bring him down here. But it was on a Thursday. Sally wasn't expecting us till next day. So when she heard voices down here in the middle of the night she came down to investigate. She was in a dressing-gown. And we were just going to explain that we'd suddenly decided to come down a day earlier than usual and brought a friend, Mr Jones, with us, when she cried out, "That's Arthur Small!" And Small made a lunge for her and would have grabbed her if I hadn't managed to get hold of one of his arms and held on to it while I yelled at her, "Get out!" And she came to her senses and ran for it. Small shook me off after only a moment – he was very strong – and went after her, but it was a very dark night and in a few minutes he came back and said she'd got away. We realized he might have caught up with her and killed her, but if he had we couldn't think how he'd hidden her body. We were all very scared. Our first idea was that she'd go straight to the police and that Small had better move on pretty quickly, so we gave him some money and he went to a hotel in Helsington. But after a few days the police hadn't come here, looking for him, and we hadn't heard any more of Sally, so we decided she must have been frightened of going to them and that it was probably safe for Small to come back here. We had the hair dye and the false moustache waiting for him by then and we installed him here as our gardener. Actually he was a very good gardener. It was the one honest thing about him.' She turned to Alison. 'I'm telling the truth. Sally bolted out of the house that evening and vanished into thin air.'

'But her luggage,' Alison said, 'and that letter she's supposed to have written. Mrs Rumbold said the luggage was gone next day and she saw the letter waiting for you. Why did you get rid of Sally's luggage and write that letter unless you knew she wasn't coming back?'

'Just to stop Mrs Rumbold raising a hue and cry for her,' Mrs Eckersall said. 'At first we only moved the luggage to the room over the garage. Mrs Rumbold hadn't got a key to it and couldn't go rummaging about in it, and the things stayed there till we were sure Sally hadn't gone to the police. Then Small put her cases in the car and dumped them in a pond or somewhere. I'd already written the letter and later I left it where I knew Mrs Rumbold would read it. What we believed after the first few days when we'd heard nothing was that Sally'd gone back to her family and that they'd advised her not to get mixed up in dangerous things. Then Mr Burnaby came down here and we heard she'd really vanished, so I started to wonder . . . Well, Small swore to us he hadn't harmed her, but if I were you, Mr Ditteridge, I think I'd find out what Jack Cassell was doing that evening.'

'You're suggesting that Cassell killed the girl for Small and disposed of her body,' the superintendent said. 'He'd have had to be told that you were going to bring Small here and have been waiting for him. Was that how it was?'

'I don't know,' she said. 'I suppose it must have been.'

'It seems to me much more likely,' Mr Ditteridge said, 'that Small killed her and bundled her body quickly into the room over the garage until he had time to bury it in this garden he was devoted to.'

'No!' both the Eckersalls exclaimed together.

Mr Eckersall went on, 'The body would have been there, wouldn't it, when we took the luggage up? But it wasn't. The room was empty. We'll all swear to that. Louise? June?'

'Yes,' they both said.

'The boot of one of the cars then.'

'No,' Mr Eckersall said. 'I looked.'

Alison could detect neither belief nor scepticism on Mr Ditteridge's face. She did not believe much of the story herself. Some of it might be true, but too many things had been left out. And why should Mrs Eckersall be so eager to tell it if it were not to cover up something more important than the things that she had admitted?

Alison's head was spinning a little and she felt a sick sort of dread. Ever since she had understood the reason why these people might want Sally dead she had felt far more frightened of what it seemed to her was about to be discovered than she had of the old blank mystery.

Mr Ditteridge also thought that too much had been left out. 'How did you become involved with Small in the first place?' he asked. 'Why did you hide him here?'

'Blackmail,' Mr Eckersall answered. 'He had something on me.'

'That you were once in prison yourself? Of course we knew that. You were investigated as soon as Miss Burnaby disappeared and you were identified as a man who'd done two years for fraud. Did you meet Small in gaol? He'd nothing on you really. You'd done your sentence and we've had nothing against you since. We haven't had much time to investigate Longthorpe Pricket, but so far as we know at present it operates quite legitimately.'

'But my clients! The very existence of my firm! Who'd trust the recommendations of a man who'd been in gaol? Because that's what we depend on, recommending the right man for the right job in the right country. So many people have fantastic daydreams about life in foreign countries and it's an important part of our work to make sure they understand the realities.' Mr Eckersall rocked backwards and forwards on the sofa in sudden excitement. 'We're only a small firm, not the grand show I sometimes like to make out, but we're doing very nicely and nothing has ever been said against our integrity, and Louise and I have built up a very good sort of life for ourselves. And think of our neighbours in a neighbourhood like this! Some day we hope to retire here. Oh, Arthur Small had me where he wanted me. And after all, it wasn't so much he wanted me to do for him. Just to provide shelter for a short time. He didn't ask for anything but shelter.'

'Didn't he ask you to smuggle him out of the country to one of those jobs you knew about?'

'Never. He never told me about his plans. He kept very much to himself.'

'That's right,' Mrs Rumbold said. 'He was a difficult man to get a word out of. Now I understand why. But blackmail – well, isn't that wicked? That's a very nasty crime.'

Alison had almost forgotten that Mrs Rumbold was there. Now Alison saw that all the fascinating information that Mrs Rumbold had acquired that morning would go circling fierily around the Good Intent, like the ball of flame seen by her friend Mrs Jellaby the evening before, spreading from the Good Intent to the Green Man and the Blue Boar and in no time at all destroying the dream of a dignified retirement for Mr and Mrs Eckersall in their charming old country house.

But perhaps they had always known that that dream had had no reality and were not much concerned at seeing it die. It was still a bit of a puzzle to Alison why they had spoken as freely as they had in front of so many people, then she thought of a possible reason why they had done it. However little they said, they were deep in trouble. But the victim of blackmail can always expect some sympathy and they had hurried to present themselves as victims. The police would perhaps deal gently with them for harbouring Arthur Small. If that was all that they had done.

Mrs Eckersall was watching Mr Ditteridge with a calculating gaze, as if she were trying to assess how the statements made by herself and her husband had affected him.

'Have you arrested Cassell?' she asked.

'Not yet,' Mr Ditteridge said.

'Why not?'

'At the moment we've nothing against him. He's got a pretty good alibi for Small's murder. The porter at the station saw them together on the platform and saw Cassell get into the train. There were very few people travelling on that trian, so the porter remembered them. The train started moving before Small walked away. It left at ten thirty-seven. You may be interested to know that Dr Murray believes Small died not much later than midnight, and at that time Cassell would still have been on the train.'

'But he could easily have jumped down on the other side of the train before it picked up speed and come straight back here and murdered Small and gone away again,' Mrs Eckersall said. 'And if that's what happened, you can stop hunting for the gun, because he'll have taken it away with him.'

'And Cassell had a motive too,' Mr Eckersall said when she stopped. Alison had never seen them so united. 'If he really was Small's accomplice in the bank robbery and got away with the money and kept it safely hidden all this time, he may not have wanted to give Small his share. If he gave it to him on his first visit, you may be sure he'll have picked it up on his second.'

Mr Ditteridge said nothing. He stood tugging at his chin and looking at the carpet. June Pullen was the first to find his silence unbearable.

'Well?' she said shrilly. 'What's wrong with that?'

'It's a nice theory,' Mr Ditteridge said thoughtfully. 'All the same, I don't think we'll stop looking for the gun yet. For one thing, we found a suitcase in Small's room with about seventy thousand pounds in it. So it looks as if he wasn't killed for the money. Cassell naturally denies knowing where it came from, but I think we'll be able to prove it this time, then he'll be arrested. Incidentally, Miss Pullen, you were in this room, were you, when Miss Burnaby recognized Small?'

'Yes,' she said.

'Why were you here?'

'I often come down here with Mr and Mrs Eckersall.'

'You knew about this blackmail, then?'

'Of course. I'm their friend as well as Mr Eckersall's secretary. I'm quite in their confidence.'

'But you didn't think it disloyal to be having an affair with the man who was blackmailing Mr Eckersall?'

Mrs Eckersall gave one of her abrupt, harsh laughs. 'Loyalty?' she said. 'That girl? Are you trying to be funny?'

Mr Eckersall reached out quickly and took one of her hands, as if he were afraid of what she might say next. She seemed ready to snatch it away, but when his tightened on it she gave him a half smile and relaxed.

June was protesting that she had never had an affair with Arthur Small and when she was told that she had been seen leaving his flat in the early morning and also that there were shreds of sticky pink fluff from her slippers in his room and traces of treacle on the slippers, she began to cry and said that she had not been disloyal to Mr Eckersall, she had only given in to Small because he had threatened to betray Mr Eckersall if she did not.

For an impromptu story it was not a bad one. Whatever he thought of it, Mr Ditteridge did not challenge her further. But Mrs Rumbold, with a sudden lewd chuckle, said, 'I've heard everything now!' She added that she thought she might as well get on with her work unless she was wanted for anything special. Mr Ditteridge allowed the gathering to break up and went out into the garden to talk to some of his men. Alison went upstairs to her room.

She could tell that the room had been searched, though it had been neatly done and all her belongings returned to almost where she had left them. She stood at the window and found that she could not stop watching the men who were digging up Barry Jones's herbaceous border. Or Arthur Small's. She was not yet used to the change of name. She did not really want to watch the men, yet she could not look away.

They were not digging up any of the older, well established plants, but only the smaller, newer plants and the annuals that had been put in recently to fill up empty spaces. In one or two places they had already dug to some depth. So it was not the gun that they were looking for. Of course it was not. From the time that the dead man had been identified as a ruthless, wanted criminal and the closeness in time been noticed between Sally's disappearance and his appearance here, the police were bound to have been thinking very seriously that he might have killed her and buried her in the garden.

The garden that Alison was sure that he had loved, whether he had buried a body in it or not. Everything else about him had been false, from the colour of his hair to his mental breakdowns, but that one passion had been genuine. Or had he only gardened perpetually out of anxiety that the earth would settle and the outlines of a grave reveal itself?

She thought of the story that the Eckersalls had told, on which they had obviously agreed beforehand, about Sally's recognition of Small and how Mrs Eckersall had held him back while Sally ran out into the darkness. It did not seem to Alison that it mattered much whether or not the story was true, for it was what had happened outside that counted. Perhaps Sally had made for the garage, to try to get out the car before Small caught up with her, but had been too slow and after all been killed, after which he had carried her body up to the flat, and later, it might even have been days later, buried her in the garden. And of course the Eckersalls had known all about it, for there had been that hasty hiding of her luggage

and the forging of the letter from her. Even if they had
briefly tried to give her a chance to escape, once she was
dead they must have been Small's accomplices.

And all because he was blackmailing them for something not a fraction as serious as murder?

Did that make sense?'

No, if all that he had on them was his knowledge that
Mr Eckersall had spent two years in prison. There would
have had to be a great deal more to it than that for them
to take the appalling risk of helping him conceal a murder.

At that point Alison remembered what Mrs Eckersall
had said to her on the subject of loyalty. She had virtually
told Alison that she had stood by her husband when he
had run into trouble and that there had been pressure on
her then to leave him, but that she had felt that this was
impossible because you could not walk out on a man when
he needed you most. In other words, Alison thought, when
he had gone to gaol. But in what way had she stood by
him? Simply by waiting for him, or had she carried out
some activities for him which would have got him a
sentence far longer than two years if they had been
discovered? Activities in which the Eckersalls had been
involved with Arthur Small.

As Alison began to believe in her own guesses she felt
a new excitement. She felt sure that at least there had
never been any blackmail. As June had cooperated, all
willingness, with Small, so also, Alison believed, the
Eckersalls had cooperated. They had willingly hidden
him. They had probably helped organize his escape from
prison. They might even have organized the robbery for
which he had gone to prison and possibly others too.
Longthorpe Pricket International Appointments Ltd.
might itself be a legitimate concern, yet it might be only
a front for very different, far more remunerative activities.

Sally had really walked into a snake pit.

But at that point Alison suddenly thought of something which, if it were true, would make nonsense of a great deal of her thinking. She was stunned by her own idea, it seemed so fantastic and yet at the same time staggeringly convincing.

Leaning on the window sill while the men in the garden dug and dug, she wondered if she was going slightly mad. Was it madness to find herself experimenting with believing both Arthur Small and Mrs Eckersall?

Just then she saw a white Volkswagen stop in the road opposite the end of the drive. A policeman went towards it, but after a moment he turned away and David Kaye came walking up the drive.

The very person Alison needed at that moment.

Not for his theories about the uses to which the garden hose had been put. It was for something far simpler.

Running downstairs and meeting him outside on the terrace, she asked him, 'David, have you got a tool kit in your car?'

'Of a sort,' he said. 'It's just about up to the job of changing a wheel.'

'Well, will you get it and come with me?' she said. 'What we want is just something to make you look workmanlike.'

He looked her in the face, seemed to see something there that made an impression on him, turned and without arguing went back to his car. Alison followed him and when he opened the boot to take out his case of tools, saw a hammer in the assorted junk that he kept there.

'Oh, take that!' she exclaimed. 'It's just what we want.'

He picked the hammer up and gave it a swing. 'Do I hit someone with it?'

'I hope it won't be necessary, but it may not be a bad thing if you look capable of doing it. Come along.'

'I came to see if the police have found out anything yet,' he said.

'A certain amount,' she answered. 'I'll tell you about it presently.' She walked to the open gate next to the Eckersalls' and started along the weed-clogged drive to the Fisks' house.

She had never been so close to it before. She had noticed from next door that for most of the time the curtains were kept drawn, but she had not noticed how tattered and soiled they were. The house itself, which had the outlines of a fine Georgian mansion, seemed to her to have a blind, scared, defensive look. She wondered if the sisters were dreadfully poor or if they were simply incapable of coping with something as practical as putting up new curtains. She also wondered if they wore their pixie hoods and tweed coats in the house. She had never seen them without them and did not even know what colour their hair was or what kind of garments the coats concealed.

There was a bell beside the door in the handsome portico and she pressed it, though without much hope that it would be in working order. Listening, she heard no sound inside the house. Trying again, she waited a little while, then grasped the tarnished lion's head on the door and pounded with it as loudly as she could.

At first she thought that this was going to bring no more response than the bell. Then she heard a sort of twittering sound on the other side of the door and realized that this was the sisters whispering to one another, probably arguing as to whether or not they should open it. Evidently they agreed that they should, for it opened a few inches and Miss Wendy peeped out. Behind her in the shadows that filled the old hall even at this hour on a sunny morning, Miss Kitty stood close to her, peering over her shoulder.

Seeing Alison, Miss Wendy stepped back, opening the door wider.

'Oh, Mrs Goodrich, how kind of you to call,' she said. 'Seeing the police still about, we wondered if we should come over to ask if you've any news, but we were afraid of being in the way. Do come in. There are so many things we'd like to ask you.'

The twins were without their hoods and coats. Both had sparse grey hair, cut short so jaggedly that it seemed plain that they cut each other's. They wore cotton blouses and tweed skirts. The blouses had once been white, but it must have been some time since they had been in the wash, for they were spotted with a variety of egg and tea stains as well as being an all-over greyish colour. The skirts had eccentrically uneven hem lines and had certainly been made at home by far from skilful hands.

Alison stepped into the hall and David followed her in.

'This is Mr Kaye,' she said. 'He came to see me this morning and it occured to me that he might be able to help you with your mirror. He's very clever with his hands and he happens to have some tools with him. I'm sure he'll be able to hang it up for you, or at least he could take a look at it and see what needs doing, then if he doesn't happen to have the right tools with him now, he could come back later and deal with it. Couldn't you, David?'

'Oh yes – yes, of course,' he said.

'How kind, how very kind!' Miss Wendy exclaimed. 'We've been at our wits' end what to do. But a stranger – we hardly like to ask you to do a thing like that for us, Mr Kaye. It's taking advantage of you. Are you sure you don't mind?'

'No trouble at all,' he said. 'Delighted if I can help.'

His voice had changed. He was no longer fumbling for the role that Alison expected him to play. He had suddenly understood why she had brought him to that house. A

look of utter disbelief appeared on his round, blunt-
featured face and at the same time a wild look of hope.
She was scared of that look of hope, because it could so
easily be doomed to change to an equally wild hurt and
despair.

'This is the mirror, is it?' he said, turning to the great
gilt-framed object that was propped against the wall at
the foot of the stairs.

The stairs must once have been beautiful. They rose in
a gracious curve to the floor above, with delicately wrought
iron banisters sweeping up beside them. But the fine
design of the metal was obscured with cobwebs and the
stair carpet was in holes.

Dust and cobwebs were dense all over the rest of the
hall, which was lofty and very dignified. A kind of grey
fluff covered the floor, through which certain pathways had
been trodden by the sisters as they went from one room
to another. One or two doors stood open, showing
magnificent rooms beyond them but all in the same state
of neglect and decay. Alison did not know which she felt
the more strongly as she looked around her, revulsion or
pity.

'Yes, that's it,' Miss Wendy said, going up to the mirror
and giving the frame a gentle stroke with her hand. 'As
you can see, it's very precious. And it's hung up there
on the wall over the stairs ever since we can remember.
We've lived here all our lives, you know. Our mother
died giving birth to us, but our father was a very wonderful
man and really gave up his life to looking after us. Very
sad, in a way, because he'd gone into parliament and was
said to have a very promising career ahead of him and he
gave up everything for Kitty and me. We were never sent
to school, he kept us at home with him and taught us
everything we know. We think of him always with the
deepest love and gratitude. That's partly why we're so

worried about the mirror. We've tried not to change anything in the house since he died. Of course we can't keep it up as he did, because for some reason servants won't stay with us and we're rather old to manage such a big house by ourselves. But we do our best, don't we, Kitty?'

'Oh yes, we always do our best,' her sister said.

'Well now, let's see what needs doing,' David said. He went a few steps up the staircase and stood looking up at the two big hooks that were fixed with plugs into the stained plaster of the wall. 'I don't think there's anything wrong with those, do you, Alison?' He glanced down at her, his look inviting her to follow him. 'They look fine and strong to me.'

She went up the stairs till she stood beside him.

'Yes, I should think they're quite all right,' she said.

'Oh yes, they are, I'm sure they are,' Miss Wendy said, a new note of agitation in her voice as Alison went another few steps up the stairs. 'It's the wire on the mirror itself that broke. That's all that needs mending, and then someone, of course, to help us lift it back on to the hooks. There's no need to go upstairs, Mrs Goodrich. Anyway, you can't reach the hooks from there, we'll have to bring in our ladder. *There's no need to go upstairs, Mrs Goodrich!*'

Her voice rose suddenly into an angry screech as Alison turned and ran as fast as she could up the rest of the stairs.

At the top she paused for an instant and looked down. David had moved to the middle of the stairs and stood firmly blocking them as the sisters tried to rush past him. She heard him say, 'Now, now,' in a good-humoured tone and saw him spread his arms to stop them passing him. The hammer in his hand perhaps frightened them, for they cowered back. Miss Kitty started to cry with loud, childish sobs.

'They'll take her away from us!' she wailed. 'And

they'll hurt her. I know they will! Oh, I can't bear it!'

Alison started to call, 'Sally!'

There was no answering call and the feeling almost of exhilaration of the last few minutes vanished in one of hopelessness and dread. But she did not wait on the first floor. On the second she paused, calling again, and this time she thought that she heard a faint call from above. But at first she could could find no staircase, leading higher. Then she found that one of the closed doors opened on to steep, narrow stairs and when she called again she heard Sally's voice, calling desperately, 'Alison – I'm here! Up here!'

As Alison ran up the stairs the ghosts of all the servants who had once slept in the attics overhead and who would have been needed to maintain the house in its ancient dignity seemed to come peeping out at her through the dust and cobwebs and to show their features in the patterns of mould that blotched the walls. There was a strong smell of mildew and the stairs were half rotten. At the top she found a narrow passage, dark, for it had no windows, and with several doors leading off it. But though they were all closed there was no need for her to try which one she wanted, for loud sounds of pounding came from behind one of them, with Sally's voice screaming at her in a frenzy, 'Alison – Alison!'

As she might have expected, the door was locked and there was no key. But at least she had found Sally.

She leant against the door, trying to get her breath after racing up all those stairs.

'Sally,' she said, 'listen, Sally – '

Sally was in no state to listen. 'Get me out!' she cried. 'Quick, get me out before they come and get you too! Oh, Alison, get me out!'

'Sally, please listen to me – '

'Open the door!' Sally shrieked. 'Open the door if you're

real! If you aren't real, go away and don't torment me. Go away, go away!'

'I'm real – oh, my dear, I'm real,' Alison said, feeling that she was going to burst out crying from sheer relief in another moment. 'And David's downstairs and there are police next door and we'll have you out in a few minutes. But we've got to get the key from those women –'

'Don't let them get near you!' Sally broke in, pounding on the door again. 'They're terrible, they're mad. Don't leave me, Alison.'

'I've got to leave you for a minute,' Alison said. 'Just while I call downstairs to David. Then I'll come back and wait here till we can get you out. I'll only be a moment, Sally. You're going to be all right.'

There was silence on the other side of the door, then Sally's voice, shaky but otherwise as Alison knew it, said quietly, 'Yes – yes, I'm all right now you're here. I can wait. But you'll stay near me, won't you?'

'I'm only going to the top of the stairs to call David.'

'All right. Yes, go.'

Alison went back along the dark passage and called. But even though the door of the attic stairs was open now, she had to go down to the next landing before David heard her. So even though the police had come into the house the day before to question the sisters about their discovery of Arthur Small's body, Sally would not have heard that they were there and would not have screamed for help, and even if by some chance in her desperation she had had an attack of screaming, they would not have heard her.

As soon as David had called back that he was coming, Alison returned to the locked door.

'Here I am again,' she said. 'You've nothing to worry about any more.'

'But that man,' Sally said uncertainly, 'the one who

tried to kill me – is he still there?'

'He's dead,' Alison said. 'There's nothing to be afraid of any more. Here's David now.'

She had heard his footsteps on the stairs. When he appeared in the dark passage she saw the key in his hand and saw how white and grim his round, pleasant face had become. She pointed at the door. He thrust the key into the lock and turned it. It made a grating sound. The moment that she heard it Sally jerked the door wide open and went straight into his arms. They clung together. sobbing meaningless things to one another, while Alison stood back and waited.

The room in which Sally had been imprisoned was a small one, lit only by a skylight. It had a bed in it with very soiled sheets and tattered blankets. There was a heavy old armchair with horsehair protruding through tears in the old green velvet that covered it. There was a table with a tin basin on it and a very old-fashioned commode, which looked as if it might be as old as the house and was probably a priceless antique.

There was also a fearful smell and though it looked as if Sally had tried to wage a war against the spiders and the mice and the mysterious grey fluff that seems to be generated by the air itself if no one disturbs it, all she had succeeded in doing was to make heaps of it in the corners of the room, heaps that looked so disgusting that it would not have surprised Alison to see them writhe into some obscene kind of life of their own.

Sally looked as if she had managed to keep herself moderately clean, except for her hair, which was a greasy tangle, and her clothes, which were only a nightdress, slippers and a blue woollen dressing-gown. She was terribly thin and the bones of her face seemed almost to show through her transparent, colourless skin. When she lifted her head from David's shoulder and looked at Alison, she saw that Sally's eyes, deep in their sockets so that she looked twenty years older than she was, had a dazed, filmed look, so that Alison feared for her sanity.

But when Sally spoke, still holding David tightly, she sounded surprisingly normal. 'How did you find me?'

'Can't that wait?' Alison said. 'We'll have plenty of time for talking presently. Now we want to get you out of here.'

'No, I want to know it now,' Sally said. 'Then I want a bath and a real meal and I want some clothes.' She managed to smile. 'I'm beginning to feel so wonderful, I can't believe it.'

'Well, I've been living next door,' Alison said. 'I'll explain about that later. I was hoping to pick up some trace of you. And this morning I heard Mrs Eckersall tell the story of how you came downstairs in the night and recognized the man they'd brought down with them as Arthur Small, the bank robber, and how he attacked you and how she held him back and you ran out into the garden. And she said Small went after you and came back after a little while and said you'd vanished. And I thought that meant he'd killed you and hidden you and then buried you later in the garden where he's been working ever since. And that's what the police think now. There are lots of them next door, digging up the Eckersalls' herbaceous border. But suddenly I thought, what would I have done if I'd been you and had had to bolt out into the night with a man who wanted to murder me chasing me? I'd have rushed straight to the house next door, of course. I'd have got the people there to take me in and hide me. And then – then I thought of how mad those women really are and that perhaps they'd kept you hidden in their house ever since. I've read of things like that happening. People have died and the neighbours have realized it and broken in and found someone hidden away in the house whom they'd never known existed. So I got hold of David and we came here together to look for you.'

'That's just what happened,' Sally said. 'Mrs Eckersall grabbed the man and shouted at me to run, and Mr Eckersall started shouting but didn't do anything, and I ran straight over here and asked the Fisks to let me come in and telephone the police. I didn't know they hadn't even a telephone. But they were very kind. They happened to be up and about, as they often are in the middle of the night, and they made me tea and said I mustn't worry about anything, they'd look after me and hide me. And that's what they've been doing ever since. I really think they half believe they've been protecting me. They've meant to be kind, that's partly what's been so awful.' Her voice began to shake ominously. 'Everything's all confused in my mind. I don't know if I'll ever manage to sort it out. I know they wanted to protect me from Arthur Small, though they said they were sure there was no one called Small around, but if ever he came back they'd make sure he never found me. Then they wanted to keep me as a sort of pet in a cage, something that was just theirs, but that they knew was just a bit dangerous, because they always came in together and blocked the doorway in case I tried to escape. I tried to at first. I thought it would be easy with two little old women like them. But they're terribly strong. You wouldn't think it to look at them, but they're made of muscle. Then I think they hated me too. They had another sister once – I think that had something to do with it. They were triplets actually, but the third one married and went away and never came back, and in some way they seemed to have me mixed up with her. She'd got away and they'd never forgiven her for it and they were going to make sure I didn't. And if you hadn't found me, if I'd stayed here much longer, I don't know – I think – I think – ' The trembling in her voice increased. 'I think I might have gone as mad as they are.'

David stroked her matted hair gently. 'Don't do any thinking you can help for the moment.' His voice was very tender. 'Lots of people get on splendidly without ever trying it.'

She rubbed her cheek against his shoulder. It looked a good solid sort of shoulder to rest on.

'D'you know, they didn't even mean to starve me,' she said. 'They eat almost nothing themselves, so they never thought I was nearly dying of hunger. And I never knew when they'd bring my tray up. It might be in the middle of the afternoon or at three in the morning. Time doesn't mean anything to them . . .' She gave a wondering little sigh. 'But it's all over, isn't it? What are we going to do now? I can't go wandering outside in a dressing-gown.'

'You can have some of my clothes,' Alison said. 'We'll go next door and you can have the bath you wanted and as much as you like to eat. But first I think we'd better have a word with Superintendent Ditteridge, so that he can tell his men to stop digging up the Eckersalls' garden. And then . . .'

'Yes, and then?' David said, looking at her curiously.

'I want a talk with Mrs Eckersall,' Alison said. 'For one thing, I want to thank her for saving Sally from Small.'

'And what else?'

She shook her head at him. She did not think that Sally was in a state to listen to a discussion of murder.

CHAPTER X

SALLY AND ALISON both talked to the police, then Mrs Eckersall helped Alison to put Sally to bed in Alison's room, which had been Sally's only a few weeks earlier. Alison tried to telephone Geoffrey, but no one answered when she rang the flat and when she rang his office she was told that he was away for the day. She guessed that he and Katrina were on their way down to Helsington.

Alison gave Sally some lunch on a tray, an omelette, some fruit and coffee, and David sat beside her while she ate. When she had finished and Alison had taken the tray off her knees, she put her hand in his and quietly went to sleep. Talking to the police had roused her for a little while and brought a too-bright flush to her cheeks, but she was in a state of intense nervous exhaustion and as soon as she had eaten she seemed simply to slip away into a deep peace. David stayed there motionless, nursing the hand that she had given him, looking almost as peaceful as she did.

Mrs Eckersall had told Alison that she would provide lunch for the rest of the household.

'If I don't, I know you'll give us eggs again and I shall vomit,' Mrs Eckersall said. 'Ever since you got here, you've given us nothing but eggs. Soufflés, scrambled eggs, bacon and eggs, omelettes. When I gave you your job you told me you could cook, but I honestly don't believe you know how to do anything but eggs.'

'The circumstances have been exceptional,' Alison said.

'Granted.' Mrs Eckersall smiled. 'Well, come down when you're ready.'

When Alison went down, however, she found that the lunch that Mrs Eckersall had taken into the dining-room and on which her husband and June Pullen had already started, consisted only of bread and cheese. Mr Eckersall was in one of his garrulous moods and said that he had felt suspicious of the two women next door from the start.

'If anyone had thought it worth while to listen to me, which they never do,' he said, 'I'd have told them to search that house from top to bottom. Your poor sister would have been saved a lot of misery.'

His wife gave him a look of weary contempt. 'You know the idea never even occurred to you.'

He leant towards Alison. 'My dear, you don't know how frustrating it is to be written off by everyone you know as a fool. I could have told you, if you'd spoken to me openly instead of coming here in the furtive way you did, that two old maniacs like that are capable of anything. Not that I'm criticizing you for deceiving us as you did, you understand. I admire you for it. I'm sure in your place I'd have done something of the same sort – '

'You wouldn't,' June interrupted fiercely. 'You'd have hidden your head in the sand, just as you're doing it now about poor Arthur. You're hoping if you pretend the murder didn't happen, it'll go away. You're not only a fool, you're a cowardly fool, that's what you are.'

'Somehow I don't think that's very respectful to your employer,' he said. 'I wonder if the time has come for your work with Longthorpe Pricket to terminate.'

'If you want to know, it's terminated already,' June said. 'How could I go on working for you after what's happened? You're a jealous, cowardly fool and I hope you pay for it.'

'It's quite extraordinary,' Mr Eckersall observed to no one in particular, 'this girl is sure I murdered Small. And out of jealousy. Me! If it was for money now, it might make some sense. I'd never murder anyone except for money. But if I'd done that, I wouldn't have left a case of the stuff up in his room, would I? Me jealous! Am I a jealous man, Louise?'

She leant back in her chair, nibbling a small piece of cheese off the end of her knife. 'No, Denis, there are very few things I can definitely say you are.'

He gave a sour grin. 'Now is that a nice thing to say? Alison, have you noticed, nobody's ever nice to me? They let me slave away to give them nice houses and nice cars and nice lady cooks and then they never even say thank you. Shall I tell you something? I've been thinking of selling up everything and going off abroad by myself, say to Australia, and starting a new life among people who haven't got the nasty habit of underrating me. I don't think I'm too old to do that. I think I might still make something of my life.'

June sprang up from her chair. 'Just try it and see what the police do to you. They're just waiting to grab you, now that Cassell's started to talk. They'll get all they need on you from him and not only for shooting Arthur. Oh God – !' Tears spurted in her eyes and ran down her cheeks. 'Why did you have to do that?'

She ran from the room.

'The bloody silly little bitch,' Mr Eckersall muttered. 'I believe she's serious. And she's out to make trouble. Why didn't those two lunatics next door collar her instead of that nice girl Sally? I suppose I'd better go and try to calm her down.'

He got heavily to his feet and, talking apparently to himself about the injustice of life, went out after June.

Mrs Eckersall and Alison sat on in the dining-room in what, by comparison, was a comfortable silence.

Then Alison said, 'I haven't thanked you yet for saving Sally that night when she recognized Arthur Small.'

Mrs Eckersall went on nibbling at her little bit of cheese before answering at last, 'Is that really all you've got to say to me?'

'We can leave it at that, if you like,' Alison said. 'We owe you more than we can ever make up to you.'

Mrs Eckersall shook her head. 'Go on and say the rest of it. We're alone. Does it matter to anyone but ourselves what we talk about?'

'Let's talk about loyalty then,' Alison suggested. 'Do you remember telling me you'd stood by a man when he ran into trouble, that there'd been pressure on you to give him up, but that you felt you couldn't just because of the trouble he was in?'

'I said all that, did I? Well, well.'

'And you said you wanted your debts paid.'

'So I do.'

'It was very stupid of me,' Alison said, 'but I took for granted the man you meant was your husband, and when I heard yesterday he'd been in prison, I thought that was the trouble you meant. And I thought your bitterness towards him was because his way of paying his debt to you was to have an affair with June. And because of that affair, I thought, you couldn't have killed Small, because his affair with June must have been a Godsend to you, as he'd taken her away from your husband.'

'What's so stupid about that?' Mrs Eckersall asked.

'Only that I'd got it the wrong way round, hadn't I? The man you were loyal to when he went to prison was Small. You stayed with your husband, though you didn't trouble to hide the fact that you disliked and despised him, because he'd the contacts to help Small to escape. And you waited for Small for three years. But when he did escape and came here to hide, he straight away started up his affair with June and that was more than you could bear. I don't know what happened on Saturday evening that was finally too much for you. Was it Cassell coming here with the money, so that Small could leave and perhaps take June with him? Did they tell you they were going away together?'

Mrs Eckersall had finished the cheese on the tip of her knife and was tapping her plate with it gently.

'You know, you could still be wrong,' she said. 'It could have been that Arthur and I were going away together and June shot him to stop it.'

'I don't think so.'

'Why not?'

'Because June visited him before it started to rain. She got treacle on her slippers. But the rain washed the treacle away into the ground. I know it did because next morning the Fisks showed me the birds' nest in the rose bush and the grass round it wasn't at all sticky. And we know Small was alive long after the rain started, because he drove Cassell to the station. So whoever killed him did it after that, perhaps even after the storm was over.'

'But why pick on me?' The soft tapping of the knife on the plate went on. 'June could have gone back.'

'And got mud on whatever shoes she wore? Don't you think the police would have been as interested in a pair of muddy shoes, if they'd found one, as in slippers with treacle on them?'

Mrs Eckersall gave a sigh. 'I know what you're going to say, of course. You're going to say I didn't get mud on my shoes because I went out barefoot. I often walk about barefoot, don't I? I remember I was doing it the very first time we met.'

'Well, didn't you? And didn't you wash the blood off your feet with the hose from the garage?'

She dropped the knife with a clatter on her plate.

'The blood?'

Alison hesitated. 'Do you really want me to go on? As

I said when we started talking, I owe you a debt and I know you like your debts paid. Believe me now, I'm ready to pay.'

'No,' Mrs Eckersall said, but her voice had gone suddenly hoarse. 'Go on.'

'Then I'll tell you what I think happened,' Alison said. 'I think you kept the gun in that walnut bureau. You went and got it and went along barefoot to the flat. The rain had stopped. Small came to the door in his dressing-gown and you shot him point blank. He collapsed in the doorway. That worried you because anyone who came by could see him. So you went into the flat past his body and tried to drag him inside so that you could shut the door on him. I suppose you were fairly sure you could make your husband help you to get rid of the body later. But you found you couldn't move it without getting blood on your clothes, so you had to leave it where it was. But you'd already got blood on your feet and made bloody footmarks on the floor. And it occurred to you that footprints are as distinctive as fingerprints and that they could easily be traced to you. So you got the hose and cleaned up the floor of the flat and washed down the steps, and while you were at it you gave Small a good soaking so that it would look as if all the wetness on the floor came from the rain having poured in. Actually it had nothing to do with creating an alibi. Then you washed your feet and hung up the hose again, only the water that was still in the hose trickled down into a small puddle on the floor of the garage and that's somehow how I thought of all this – water – your bare feet – blood. I was worried by that puddle from the time I saw it.'

Mrs Eckersall nodded musingly. '"The element of water moistens the earth,"' she observed, '"but blood flies upwards and bedews the heavens . . ." Don't look so surprised. I do read sometimes. Webster, isn't it? What that man knew about hatred and treachery! Do you know, this morning I sat looking out at the dawn? That isn't a thing I often do. With the sleeping pills I take I don't usually raise an eyelid till my breakfast comes in. But last night I didn't take any pills. They wouldn't have worked anyhow, and I didn't want to sleep. And when I saw the dawn, a sort of dirty red along the horizon, I thought it looked as if some great big finger had smeared blood along it . . . But what did I do with the gun?'

'I don't know.'

Mrs Eckersall gave a dry little laugh. 'Thank God there's something you don't know. Of course you've no proof of any of this.'

'No.'

'But you'll go to the police with it all the same.'

'Would that be paying my debt?'

Mrs Eckersall's wide eyes looked at her wonderingly. 'Are you serious about that?'

'I'm perfectly serious. But I'll tell you something. I think, even if I say nothing, they'll work all this out for themselves sooner or later. Now that they can stop digging up the garden, looking for Sally, they'll be tearing that flat apart and the chances are there'll be traces of footprints you missed. Or there'll be something else. For one thing, your husband may talk. He must know what's happened, and although I don't believe he'll have to give evidence against you, I shouldn't trust him too far. So I'd think very carefully about what you should do.'

'What do you think I should do?'

Mrs Eckersall had become curiously impersonal, almost as if she were an interrogator conducting some kind of official inquiry and it was Alison who was under suspicion.

'I suppose it depends on how you feel,' Alison said.

'How do you think I should feel?'

'I don't know. I don't know how it feels to have killed one's lover.'

'Part of you dies with him,' the other woman answered. 'Another part hates him still as much as you did when you pulled the trigger.' For an instant a look of violence blazed on her face, violence such as she had said that she had hated in her father. Then she added almost indifferently, 'But part of you seems to have no feelings at all. I don't much care what happens to me.'

'That's how you feel at the moment. You may feel differently tomorrow.'

Mrs Eckersall closed her eyes, withdrawing deeply into herself. Her face had a parched look now, as if the blood supply to it had run dry. After a moment, opening her eyes, she gave another sigh.

'There are several things I could do,' she said. 'I could wait till tomorrow then take the car and drive off into the blue. I don't suppose the police would have enough against me by then to stop me.'

'Someone would follow you, all the same.'

She shrugged her shoulders. 'Anyway, I don't know where I'd go. Perhaps I'd drive over the edge of a cliff. D'you know of any good cliffs anywhere near? Or I might look for the gun, if I could find it again, and shoot myself. Or I might even confess. What about that? Would that be a good idea?'

Alison said nothing. The fact that there was mockery in Mrs Eckersall's voice did not delude her. She was struggling painfully to arrive at her true feelings.

'Some people who've committed murders have gone into convents for the rest of their lives, haven't they?' she said. 'I seem to have read about that. I shouldn't think a modern prison is much worse than a convent. There'd be no problems, no responsibilities, though I believe the food isn't specially good. And you'd have your thoughts, of course, and no chance to drown them in drink. That might make things difficult. I think I'll have a drink now. I may be able to think more clearly when I've had one or two.'

She stood up. She looked so tired, it seemed to be a great effort for her to drag herself on to her feet. She walked slowly to the door. Turning there, she looked at Alison again.

'I believe we might have got along very well, you and I, if we'd had time to get to know one another better. I believe you rather like me, even if you think you ought not to. You see a bit of yourself in me, perhaps. But I'm an evil woman and you've never even known what it is to be tempted. You'd never be capable of falling in love with a man you knew was worthless.'

Questions of good and evil always tended to embarrass Alison. She still remained silent.

'Give my regards to that husband of yours when you see him,' Mrs Eckersall went on. 'I never believed he'd left you, you know. You've never had the look of someone who'd had to give up all they've ever cared about. Now I'll have that drink. Will you join me?'

Alison never knew what she might have answered, for at that moment she heard the sound of a shot and an inhuman scream.

The scream was in fact not human. It had issued from the throat of the ginger tom and when she ran out into the garden she saw the animal lying under a tree by the fence between the Fisks' garden and the Eckersalls'. Miss Kitty was standing a little way off with a revolver in her hand. Her sister was beside her. Both of them were wearing their pixie hoods and tweed coats and were carrying ancient but splendid leather suitcases.

One of the policemen, evidently a cat lover, ran to the cat and gathered it up gently into his arms. It gave another great yowl at being touched, so it was not dead. There was a good deal of blood, but from the way that it squirmed in the man's clasp, it looked as if it had not been very seriously injured.

Mr Ditteridge, more diffidently, advanced on Miss Kitty, holding out his hand. She put the gun into it without any hesitation. She had no designs on human life.

'What a pity she missed him, isn't it?' Miss Wendy said to Alison. 'They're taking us away, you see, I'm not sure where, so we thought for the sake of those dear little birds we'd better kill the horrid creature before we left. And Kitty's aim is usually so good. She's managed to drive him away with stones more than once. I don't know why she missed him just now. Perhaps she's nervous. Our dear father taught us to shoot, you know, among a lot of other useful things.'

'But where did you get this gun?' Mr Ditteridge asked with wonder on his face. He looked more disturbed than Alison had ever seen him.

'Why, we found it in the rose bush yesterday morning just before we found poor Mr Jones's body,' Miss Wendy answered. 'We were looking at the nest to see if the eggs had hatched yet and there the lovely little birds were, all with their beaks open, crying to be fed. And the gun was on the ground, almost underneath the nest. I suppose the murderer must have thrown it down there after shooting Mr Jones. It's quite a miracle he didn't hit the nest. Wonderful, really.'

'And it never occurred to you to give us the gun?' Mr Ditteridge said. 'Don't you know we've been hunting for it all yesterday and today?'

'Have you really? I'm so sorry.' Her tone was one of mild apology, as if at some insignificant social error. 'We thought we'd keep it because you never know when a thing like that may come in useful.'

'No, indeed. Now if you're ready, Miss Fisk, the car's waiting.'

'Oh, we're quite ready,' she said. 'So good of you to drive us.'

Close together as always, with Miss Wendy a little in the lead, the sisters set off down the drive.

Mr Ditteridge turned to Alison.

'Tragic business,' he said. 'They've always been thought of as harmless eccentrics, but it's got to be faced after what they did to your sister, they're dangerous.'

'Where are you taking them?' Alison asked.

'First to the police station,' he said. 'Then it'll be over to the psychiatrists, thank God. Nothing more to do with me. How's your sister feeling now?'

'She's sleeping.'

'Oh, Mr Ditteridge – '

It was Mrs Eckersall's voice. It made Alison start, because she had taken for granted that Mrs Eckersall had followed her out, but now she realized that the other woman was only just approaching along the terrace. Her walk was unsteady and her words were slurred.

'Mr Ditteridge,' Mrs Eckersall repeated carefully, looking at him vaguely as if from a great distance. In fact she was already very far away from them all. 'I've decided I may as well tell you I killed Arthur Small. Ask Mrs Goodrich if – if you want to know – ' Her knees buckled under her and she would have fallen to the ground if one of the men standing there had not caught her. Just before her eyes rolled upwards and she slumped in his arms, unconscious, she muttered what sounded like, ' – the details.'

Alison saw the sunlight flash on the great diamond on her finger and wondered which of the men had given it to her, Arthur Small or Denis Eckersall. Or had she

bought it for herself? Perhaps that was the likeliest thing
to have happened.

Louise Eckersall died that evening. She had had the
drink that she had said she wanted, half a bottle of whisky,
drunk straight down, on top of all the barbiturates that
she had had in her bathroom cabinet. In the hospital
they worked on her for hours, but she had made sure
that they would have no chance of saving her.

By then Jack Cassell had done all the talking that was
needed and Denis Eckersall and June Pullen were
arrested the same evening for their part in the bank
robbery that had sent Arthur Small to prison and for
helping in his escape.

Geoffrey and Katrina had arrived from London in the
afternoon. Sally had woken up, dressed in some of Alison's
clothes and met them in the drive. There had been cries
of excitement, embraces, some tears. They had wanted
her to go back to London with them, but she had put
her hand in David's and said that she was staying with
him. He and she had driven off to his caravan.

Geoffrey and Katrina went back to London. Alison
went to a hotel in Helsington. The police wanted her to
stay on because they wanted to take a statement from her.
Late in the evening Mr Ditteridge came to tell her that
Mrs Eckersall had died. He said that the statement
could wait till the morning.

'I'd go straight to bed now, if I were you,' he said.
'You look ready to drop.'

Alison felt ready to drop. But there was one thing she
wanted to do before she went to bed. She went up to her
room, sat down at a table and started a letter, 'My
darling Mark . . .'

She paused there. She had imagined that what she
had to say to him would come pouring out in a compulsive
flow of words that would take hardly any thought, but

all that she could think of just then was Mrs Eckersall telling her to give him her regards.

In the end Alison wrote a very short letter in which she only told him that she loved him and needed him. She felt better when she had done that, but she tore the letter up in the morning, for it did not sound very rational and it might worry him, deep in his rain forest, to receive a letter like that. It occurred to her as she sat there pondering that she had no idea how much it rained in a rain forest. Enough to wash away treacle, blood, guilt?

The letter that she ought to send him, she thought, was a simple, factual account of everything that had happened during the last few days. But when she tried to write this, she found it so difficult that she tore up all her attempts at it and in the end more or less rewrote her first brief letter.